META

Tom Reynolds

"Any sufficiently advanced technology is indistinguishable from magic."
Arthur C. Clarke

ONE

Jones and The Governor are the topic of today's lesson at St. Albert's High School, where I am sitting quietly in my 10th grade social studies classroom. Everyone in the classroom is trying to pretend that they're not looking at Connor Connolly. The new kid with the dead parents. Me.

Seeing if I'll cry.

Or get angry.

Or run out of the classroom.

Any of the things you'd expect a teenager to do when they have to sit through a history lesson about the event that claimed his parents' lives. I wasn't used to this back home. Back home, I was one of a dozen kids in every class who had lost someone in The Battle. Not the case here in Bay View City.

My brother was twelve years older than me, but still barely an adult when everything happened. Even though I'm only two years away from being eighteen myself, I cannot even begin to imagine what it would be like to have to suddenly raise a six-year-old on your own.

He did the best he could with what he had, and what he had was a small cash settlement from the United States government. A pittance of an apology for their inability to protect citizens from metahumans gone rogue.

It was the last day of classes and everyone was busy figuring out their summer plans. Well, I say figuring out, but really, almost everyone knew what they were doing. Today was more about sharing their plans, seeing whose were the most impressive. No one asked me what my plans were.

After school, I returned home to find my brother Derrick was just waking up.

"Rough night?" I ask.

"Something like that," he replies.

Derrick is a reporter. Well technically, he's a blogger but

don't ever correct him about that. As far as he's concerned, there's absolutely no difference between the two. I'm acutely aware the major difference is that one pays an actual salary and the other does not.

Since Mom and Dad died Derrick has been obsessed with metahumans. Luckily the site he works for, The Rodgerson Post, is just as obsessed with them. Derrick is probably one of the world's foremost authorities on metahumans, which in many fields could land him a very lucrative job. However, he's also probably one of the internet's foremost metahuman conspiracy theorists. Considering the majority of the conspiracy theories around metahumans concern government cover-ups of the deaths of tens of thousands of citizens, you can see how this is something we'd call a "job liability". Sleeping until three p.m. everyday is another one. Luckily, they let him work from home whenever he wants.

"We'd gotten an anonymous tip that a metahuman was sighted down by the old power station two nights ago. Turned out to be nothing," he says.

"Of course it was nothing. There hasn't been *something* in over 10 years," I tell him.

"You don't really believe all of that horseshit do you? You know that some of them are still out there, hiding," Derrick says.

"Yes, I do believe that 'horseshit', because if some of them were still out there, then why do you think we haven't actually, you know, *seen* them." I'm not even sure why I'm willing to get into this argument again. We must have had it a million times, and it's not like I'm going to change Derrick's mind.

"God. Open your eyes Connor. You think it's a coincidence that just when the government learns how to kill a metahuman they all just disappear? I don't understand how you can be so naive." Derrick says.

"I don't understand why everything has to be so complicated. Is it really that hard to believe that all the bracelets just stopped working?" I asked.

The truth is; no one really knows what happened. Out of the dozen metahumans that the world had come to know, only a few were actually confirmed dead. The Governor was, of course, confirmed dead by the government (don't bring this up around Derrick unless you want to be lectured for a half hour about how blind to the truth you are). Jones was basically assumed dead, and anyone that remembers the blast had little reason to question it. Metahumans might have seemed pretty tough, but it's impossible for all but the most delusional to believe that anyone could have survived that blast.

Most of the others died of stupidity well beforehand. To be fair, their accidents were really only stupid in retrospect. It's not like the metabands came with instruction manuals. Most of them died before they even had a chance to come up with their own crime-fighting name.

Ralph Smith died when he teleported himself to the basement of Fort Knox, intent on stealing the nation's gold reserves. The only problem was; there is no basement in Fort Knox. They found the very top of his head peaking out through the solid concrete floor in the vault. He'd fused with the floor itself.

After his unfortunate example, others with the power to teleport did so much more carefully, only transporting themselves to places they'd been before and were confident hadn't physically changed since their last visit. Of the four known teleporters that were now M.I.A. it was impossible to know how many might be stuck in a wall somewhere, explaining why we hadn't heard much from them lately.

Elaine DeGrasse was another famous metahuman, Darwin Award winner. Her metabands were in her possession for all of about 3 minutes before her untimely passing. Not nearly enough time for the cuffs to adapt to her physiology. Elaine had always dreamt of flying, and when given the chance to do so with her newly discovered "magical" bracelets, she did not hesitate. Off she went, blasting into the air with a speed no one had ever witnessed before.

What she didn't understand; was that metabands did not necessarily come with the ability to overcome the basic human need for something called oxygen. On a clear night, and with a strong telescope, you can still see her asphyxiated body orbiting the Earth.

"By the way, I'm not going to be able to give you a ride to school tomorrow. Car's in the shop," Derrick informs me.

"I don't have school tomorrow. Today was the last day of classes," I tell him.

"Wait, today was? Oh wow, it's June isn't it? Alright, school's out! Right buddy?" Derrick says in his best attempt at feigning enthusiasm, punching me in the arm a little too hard. "So what are the big plans for your first night of freedom tonight?"

"Freedom" as a sixteen-year-old doesn't mean a whole hell of a lot. What "freedom" essentially boiled down to for me and everyone else I know, is the option of either staying at home to play video games until your eyes fell out, or going to the woods to drink warm, cheap beer with a bunch of idiots whose sole purpose in life seems to be informing you of "how wasted" they are.

Neither of these appeal to me tonight, or ever really. Despite Jim's assurances to the contrary, tonight will likely end with Jim and I walking around the neighborhood bored out of our minds before we inevitably end up at a diner eating chicken fingers. Same old, same old. Jim's my best friend, and by best friend, I mean he's my only friend.

Generally speaking, Jim's slightly more outgoing than I am. Or at least slightly more interested in seeming to be part of the actual general population of the school itself. It can be annoying at times, but at the end of the day, he's still a great friend. He's never let me down and is always game for just about anything. Unfortunately tonight, anything means going to the woods to drink warm beer with the popular kids.

Well, in all likelihood it'll be more like watching the popular kids drink lukewarm beer while we sit on tree stumps. Neither of us have a way to get beer (nor am I really interested in the first place), and the kids throwing parties like this aren't exactly known for picking up a few extra cases of beer just in case the unpopular kids, who weren't invited, show up. At sixteen, anyone who can get beer is basically looked up to as metahuman themselves.

"I don't think I really want to go," I say to Jim.

We're at his house, playing video games until our eyes fall out. Jim sighs.

"This again? Come on, man," he says.

"What do you mean; this again?" I say.

"This. The whole 'too cool for school' routine. It's getting old man," Jim says.

"Old? Old to who?" I say.

"Old to me, who coincidentally is the only one who'll ever be around for it to get old to if you don't come out of your shell a little bit," he says.

"I'm not in a shell," I lie to him.

"Yes you are. When's the last time you've been to a party?" he asks.

"You mean a real party or one of these lame 'let's all talk about how wasted we are in the woods get-togethers?" I ask back.

"Oh, I didn't realize that woods parties were beneath you all of a sudden. Surely, you must have other, much more exciting, plans tonight Mr. Bond. Shall I send the helicopter to fetch you from your penthouse afterwards, so we can get chicken fingers at the diner?" he asks.

This actually does make me laugh.

"Seriously though dude, it's the last day of class. Relax a little bit for God's sake. Is one party in the woods going to kill you?" he asks.

"Who knows, it might. What if there are bears?" I ask

back sarcastically.

"I give you a zero bears guarantee. And on top of that, I give you a 100% percent Sarah Miller guarantee," he tells me.

"Why would I care?" I lie to him again.

The reason I would care, of course, is because I like Sarah Miller. Like, like her. You'd have to be literally insane not to like Sarah. She's funny, beautiful, and probably one of the smartest girls in our class. The only thing keeping every guy in our class from falling madly in love with her; is probably that she's too smart to ever really like any of them back. Guys my age don't like funny girls. There's something about the mind of a sixteen-year-old male that makes most of us put girls in either the "hot" or "nerd" category. Sarah's smart, so that overrides everything and puts her in the nerd category for most. Not me though.

"Don't say anything in front of her, all right? I really don't need that kind of aggravation tonight Jim,"

"Would you relax already? What are you so afraid of that I'm going to say?" he asks.

"Uhh, probably something along the lines of 'Hey, Sarah, did you know that Connor is insanely in love with you even though he'll never admit it?' like you did literally two weeks ago in front our entire social studies class." I reply.

"Those were crazy times, Connor. I've grown a lot as a person since then. You should know that," he replies.

He hasn't, but still, if there's a chance Sarah's going to be there, it might just be worth the risk of public humiliation.

TWO

"How far is this thing? We've been walking for thirty minutes now," I complain to Jim.

"Are you going to be like this the entire time? Unless you've forgotten, it's not exactly legal to throw an underage kegger in the woods. Everyone got busted a few weeks ago so they had to move it. We're almost there," Jim tells me.

Jim has had his head down for at least the last ten minutes now, fixated on his smartphone screen. We're following the tiny pulsating blue dot to the party of the century. Somehow, I have a feeling that I am going to be disappointed.

"Stop making that face," Jim says without looking up from his phone.

"What face? I'm not making any face," I say.

"The pissed off, 'I'd rather be anywhere on Earth but here' face. I don't need to look at you right now to tell that you've got it on," he says.

"How much further?" I ask.

"Are we there yet? I have to go potty!" Jim mocks. "Wait, do you hear that?"

We stop in our tracks and can hear the distant pumping of bass and what sounds like the chattering of a crowd. It's the party, and it can't be far from where we are.

"Come on," Jim says as he begins hurrying his pace.

We reach the party and while it pains me to admit it to Jim, he's right. This is no middle of the woods kegger. This is a full blown rave. What Jim's confidential party sources didn't inform him about; was that this is actually the party of Adam Felder, a graduating senior and the spoiled son of very rich, and also very absentee parents.

There were strobe lights, (cold) beer and an actual honest-to-God DJ. Adam and his rich buddies had hitched a generator to one of their ATVs and brought all of this stuff out into the woods yesterday to begin setting up. No wonder it was set so deep. Any closer to civilization and the cops were certain to have found it. One thing was for sure: this was definitely not my scene, nor do I belong here.

"Calm down man, it's fine. The entire school is here. Grab a beer and relax! It's summertime!" Jim tries to convince me.

"Hey! Ralph! Ralph! I can't believe it, that's Ralph! We went to kindergarten together! This is crazy. Ralph!" Jim yells above the thumping music as he wanders off.

Great. Now I'm completely alone at a party I'm not even invited to.

"Where's your friends, Professor No-Friends?" A voice behind me asks. Thirty seconds into this party, and I'm already about to get bullied. Even better. I swing around with half a "just leave me alone" already loaded into the barrel of the proverbial comeback gun when I see who said it. It's Sarah. And she's smiling. I'm immediately and completely dumbfounded by just how absolutely adorable she is when she smiles. I stand there thinking about this without saying anything for what I'm sure is an uncomfortable amount of time. It was a joke, I guess?

"I'm just messing with you," she says.

It was a joke. Ha. Yes, of course.

"I don't think I've ever seen you out at one of these before. Didn't think they were really your thing," she tells me.

"Oh, well, yeah, I mean usually they're not, but you know, it's the last day of school so I figured why not mix it up a bit?" I manage to stammer out.

'Mix it up a bit'? Who do I think I am? I don't talk like that. I don't think anyone actually talks like that. I am officially an idiot, and my true inner idiot seems to really come out and shine whenever Sarah is around.

"Well it's cool that you're here! Never thought I'd see the day. Can I get you a beer or something?" she asks.

'Can I, Sarah Miller, get you, Conner Connolly, a beer?' I think to myself. What the hell is going on. Am I in some type of alternate universe where everything is like real life but opposite?

"Uh, yeah, sure," I blurt out.

"Cool, what do you drink?" she asks.

"Ah, ya know. The hard stuff," I say.

'The hard stuff'? I am losing my mind. What the hell does the hard stuff even mean? I've heard it in movies before, sure, but I'm not actually sure what that is. Is it more solid? Like a milkshake or something? Did I just ask her for a beer milkshake? Does that make me sound incredibly sissy?

"Oh, I don't know if they have any liquor here, actually," she tells me.

Right! Liquor. That's what the hard stuff is. I knew that.

"Ah, too bad. Whatever you're having is cool then," I tell her.

"Great, I'll be right back," she says as she walks off into the crowd.

Did I actually manage to sound cool just there. Maybe I did. 'I'll take whatever you're having.' That does sound pretty cool, I guess. What if what she's having is girly though? What if she comes back and hands me a pink drink in a martini glass with one of those little umbrellas in it? I can't insult her by not drinking it, can I? I guess I'll just have to cross that bridge when I come to it.

"What the shit do you think you're doing here?"

Before I even turn around, I know who the words have come from. Brad Turner. One of Adam Felder's football teammates. I don't think Brad even knows my name, but that hasn't stopped him from trying to make my life a living hell for the past year. I turn around and can tell by the way he's swaying that he's already had too much to drink.

"Seriously Connolly. Who do you think you are, man? Were you even invited?" He asks me.

Huh. He does know my name after all.

"It's the last day of school, I thought everyone was invited," I tell him.

"Everyone was invited. You're not everyone though. You're

nobody, so you're not invited," he tells me in probably the most creative wordplay he's ever put together.

"Funny," I say.

"Seriously bro. You're not invited, get out of here. If Adam sees you, he's gonna flip," Brad says.

"It's a party in the middle of the woods. No one's supposed to be here," I say.

"This is your last warning, bro," he threatens.

I look through the crowd to see if I can spot Sarah, trying to decide which is the worse fate: leaving without even saying goodbye and looking like a total jerk, or staying so she can come back just in time to see three meatheads pummeling me. Of course, I choose the path of least embarrassment and leave with my tail between my legs.

Walking back through the woods, I've never felt this particular type of shame. What was I supposed to do though? Take a beating like a man? Fight back against three Neanderthals? All that would do is infuriate them more. The physical bruises I can take, but I just can't be humiliated like that in front of the entire school. Not again.

On my walk back, I think a lot about my parents. What they would have thought of the person their six year-old son has become. Dad was never a fighter, but he had at least seemed to have that particular gift of charm that allowed him to talk his way out of nearly any situation. At least that's what Derrick tells me. I don't remember that type of stuff myself. All I can remember is how strong he seemed to me as a kid, like nothing could ever possibly hurt him. Not even forty-three stories of concrete and steel.

I like to think Mom would be proud of me, no matter what, but I know deep down that I only feel that way because she was my mom. They're supposed to be proud, even if their kid turns out to be a loser who can't even form three coherent sentences in front of a member of the opposite sex. Maybe at least, she would have been able to give me some advice about how to not simultaneously come off as both a creep and a weirdo to literally any girl I find even mildly attractive.

The woods seem darker now than they had when Jim and I started our trek out here. The full moon has disappeared behind the clouds. Am I even going the right way? The trees in front of me look familiar, but I suppose that's only because they are trees. All trees look familiar to if you stare at them long enough in almost, pitch-black darkness.

I hear something off in the distance. An animal? Yeah, probably just an animal. I remember specifically requesting reassurance from Jim that there were no bears out here.

I keep walking, a little bit quicker now. I hear it again. Is it human? It can't be. Maybe it is and it's just from the party. No, there's no way. The party is at least fifteen minutes in the other direction. I can't hear the music any more, so there's no way I'd be able to actually hear a person.

Another scream.

Okay. That is definitely a person. I can hear it more distinctly now. It was a cry. It could be one of those weird animals that sounds like a person. The way a crying cat can sometimes sound almost exactly like a baby. But it's not a cat. Something is wrong, I can feel it.

I don't know what I can do but I know there's one thing that I can't do, and that's live with myself if I simply ignore what is obviously the sound of someone in trouble. Maybe it's someone from the party? Maybe they're hurt? Maybe it's Sarah. Maybe she came after me once she heard I was kicked out, but fell and twisted her ankle on a dead tree branch. I could swear the party is still in the other direction, but to be honest, I'm completely turned around and really have no idea.

The cries are getting louder as I approach but it still seems far away. As I get closer though, I can hear words. One word in particular: "help" in between weeping. What is going on? I still can't see where the calls are coming from but I'm scared. I reach into my pocket to get my phone. There's actually a signal. This small comfort assures me, that at the very least, I'm not inside a horror film.

I call 911 and wait. What if I'm wrong? What if it's just someone playing a prank and now I'm the buzzkill that called the cops into the woods, who will surely find the party and at the very least, shut it down, if not arrest Adam and his friends. The thought paralyzes me for a second before I hear a click and the operator on the other end.

"911, what's your emergency?" The operator asks over the phone.

"Hi. Um, I'm not sure what my emergency is, but I'm in the woods and I can hear someone crying for help," I say into the receiver.

"The woods? Can you be more specific sir?" she asks.

"Near mile marker, forty-two on Old Brooksville Highway. Maybe about a ten minute walk north," I say.

"And your reason for being in the woods, sir?" she asks.

Damn. I hadn't thought about that.

"Uhh, hiking," I say.

"Hiking? It's nearly midnight, sir," she states plainly.

"Night hiking. Listen, I think this person's in trouble, you have to send someone out here," I say.

"Can you see where the cries for help are coming from, sir?" she asks.

"No, I cannot," I say.

"Okay sir, stay on the line please. We do have a Missing Child alert active right now in your vicinity, so we are dispatching a unit immediately," she says.

"How long will it be?" I ask.

"They are ten minutes away from your location," she tells me.

A blood curdling scream rips through the quiet night air. Whoever this is, they're in trouble. And they're close.

"Did you hear that?" I ask.

"No sir. Please just stay put and a unit will be there as soon as they possibly can," the operator says.

No way. Ten minutes just to get here by car. It'll take another five minutes on foot, even if they're running, and if they're heading in the right direction. I can't be sure of that.

"I have to get closer. I can't wait that long. This person sounds like they're in trouble," I tell the operator.

"Sir. Please. This could be a dangerous situation. I need you to stay right where you are," she says to empty air.

I won't be able to live with myself if there's something terrible happening down there and I did nothing to stop it. Whatever it is, I realize it's not a good idea to head down there alone with my phone making any noise. I knew I should have read those instructions and figured out how the mute function works. I reluctantly hit the End Call button and begin walking towards where I last heard the screams.

One thing about being quiet while walking through the woods at night: it's very hard to be quiet while walking through the woods at night. It's like every single, dry leaf and dead branch found a way to form a path exactly in the direction I am heading. I don't even actually know where I'm heading any more.

The crying stops. Suddenly, the lack of crying or screams is scarier than when they sounded like they were only fifty yards away. I feel all alone in the woods. Why did the crying stop? Who made it stop and how did they do it? I begin to feel sick to my stomach.

That's when I see her through a clearing up ahead. A young girl, no older than six, I imagine. She's lying on the ground. Her hands and feet are bound together and a dirty rag is stuffed in her mouth. Even from half a football field away, I can see that her face is slick with tears. She locks eyes with me and I've never seen someone so afraid in my life. Someone has planned something awful for this poor, innocent little girl and I run towards her in the hopes that maybe I can do something to stop it in time.

Kneeling down, I begin tearing at the knots. The rope is thick and these are not traditional knots. I can't tell which piece is tied to what and begin just pulling at them at random, desperately hoping some of them, any of them, will begin to loosen up.

The little girl's crying has stopped. I think for a moment that maybe she's just all cried out and look up to reassure her. Her eyes are looking past me, I notice, a brief moment before I feel intense, sharp pain in my back and the warmth of my own blood beginning to soak my shirt.

THREE

I can't see who did this. He must have hit a major organ, or artery because the world begins closing itself off to me fast. My vision becomes a tunnel and sounds are now far away, deep down that tunnel. I slump over and feel a moment of temporary relief. At least the knife isn't inside me any more.

In another moment, I feel the blood around me. Wet and sticky at the same time. A thought occurs: this much blood cannot be outside my body. Even if someone found me now, even if they stopped the bleeding, there's no way my body could keep functioning with this much blood outside of it. I'm dying and there's nothing that can be done.

Derrick. Oh no. Poor Derrick. He'll never forgive himself for this. When Mom and Dad died, he swore he'd look after me. Keep me safe. He's already so close to the edge, so affected by their deaths, that he may never come back from this.

I'm sorry Derrick, I apologize as tears begin streaming down my face, pooling together with the growing puddle of blood forming under my body. And that poor, little girl. I failed. I can't hear her cries any more. I'm not sure if it's my losing consciousness, or if that monster used the knife he killed me with on her. I stop even caring about the fact that I'm dying, all that matters in my mind right now, is that I couldn't save her.

I gather my last bit of strength and lift my head. It feels like it weighs a thousand pounds, and the rest of me feels paralyzed. Slowly, my dying body begins to cooperate, and I can see past myself. The little girl is no longer there. Maybe she ran. Maybe, somehow I did manage to untie one of those knots, and she took the opportunity to make a break for it. It's almost impossible, but I can hope.

Everything is becoming very dark now, but I'm no longer scared. I begin to close my eyes as I see my father standing over me. He looks just as I remember him all those years ago. There's blood in the back of my throat as I say three words before I close my eyes.

"I'm sorry, Dad."

He smiles at me and says, "it's okay, son. You did good."

FOUR

Crickets are chirping. A gentle early summer breeze blows over my face. For a moment, I forget that I'm dead and just lay there enjoying it. Just for a moment before my memories rush back to me, and I remember what happened. My eyes snap open. Leaves and wilderness. I'm right where I died.

"Is this heaven?" I wonder. Maybe I'm a ghost. That makes a lot of sense if ghosts really are souls with unfinished business left on earth. I try to sit up and feel horrific pain in my back. Guess I'm not a ghost.

I'm alive. How long was I out for? It feels impossible to tell. Was it a minute or hours? Surely it couldn't have been that long considering how badly I am bleeding. One singular thought occurs to me, regardless of what is happening, I need to get up. Now.

I try to sit myself up again and just now feel that my arms are pinned down. They're out to my side and feel impossible to lift. I try to turn my head to look at them, but even this hurts worse than any pain I'd ever felt before. I strain one more time to sit up but again, my arms prevent me from doing so.

I concentrate on my right hand. Putting every last ounce of strength that I have left into just trying to pick it up. What is holding me down? Did the man return to shackle me in the middle of the night? Now that I think about it, my right wrist feels cold, almost like it is wrapped in steel. I feel my chest and arm muscles burning as I strain. It feels as though I am going to dislocate my shoulder or tear a muscle. None of that matters though, especially if today is going to be my last day on Earth, anyway.

As if a rubber band snaps, my arm frees itself from the ground. It feels like a magnet's switched polarity and now, whatever it is that was holding my arm down, is instead flinging it in the other direction, across my chest and onto my left arm.

The last thing I remember is hearing a metallic clang. Like two medieval swords smashing into each other, only a hundred times louder. For a long moment, I feel nothing at all. The pain is gone. It is as if for the first time since I was in the womb, my body feels entirely neutral. Reset back to factory settings. Then it happens.

At first, it feels like a mild electric shock. Like when you accidentally put your finger on one of the prongs of an electrical plug as you're shoving it into the wall behind a couch. It takes a moment to realize that it's electricity moving its way up your body. Not a painful feeling, necessarily but entirely unpleasant in its unnaturalness. I stand up.

All pain is gone and I now feel better than I ever have in my life. I can feel every cell in my body as though they're waking up for the first time ever. All of my senses are heightened. The woods are alive with seemingly a million different sounds, and I can now differentiate them all. The full moon illuminates the surrounding forest like a spotlight, and I can see through the foliage for miles in either direction. Right about now, I also realize that I am no longer standing, but rather hovering a meter above the grassy earth.

Yes, hovering. I let out a brief yelp. My body does that involuntary twitch thing, like when you're starting to fall asleep and dream that you're falling. Once I relax though, my body slowly descends back to solid ground, which I'll admit is very much a relief. That's when I first see them.

Metabands. Silver and seamless. The finish is dull and non-reflective. Even under the bright full moon, they're hard to see, but there they are. And they are on my wrists.

This is impossible. Maybe I am dead after all. That was a lot simpler of an explanation than why I am now standing, and only a moment ago hovering, in the forest with metabands on my wrists. These shouldn't exist. They haven't existed in a decade. Not functioning ones anyway. There was no possible way on Earth that I could be wearing metabands.

And yet I am.

The little girl.

I'm so busy admiring my new fashion accessory, that I have almost completely forgotten about that poor little girl. Well to be fair, I am also marveling at just how not dead I am, which is also quite a spellbinding of a mystery, although not as unbelievable, considering I am wearing bracelets that had made some nearly immortal.

Was she still alive? I still don't know how much time has passed. Have I been out twenty minutes, or have I been asleep for days while the metabands slowly brought me back from the brink of death? And most importantly, how did these find their way around my wrists in the first place?

Now isn't the time to ask these questions, though. A terrified young girl was somewhere in this forest with a very dangerous man. At least hopefully she was still here. But which way? That's when I hear a small muffled cry. It sounds as though it came from right beside me. I quickly look to the right, but there is nothing but woods for miles. So I begin to run.

Running feels strange. Effortless. I am moving faster than I've ever moved before in my life. *Moving* faster, not just running faster than I've ever ran before. I feel like there's a jet engine strapped to my back. Trees pop up into my path, but I move around them with complete ease. Even though I am running at what must be at least a few hundred miles per hour, it feels as though everything is in slow motion. The entire world had slowed down just to make running at this incredible speed easier for me. My amazement ends when I smash directly into a maple tree.

Except I hardly feel it. The tree explodes into a flurry of splinters and saw dust, but I wouldn't have even noticed if I hadn't been looking when it happens. I run through another. And another, delighting in how it sounds like gigantic baseball bats cracking. I stop dodging trees altogether and begin just plowing through them at full speed. That is until I reach the clearing. And them.

They're both still at least a mile away from me across a field of tall grass, but I can see them clear as day.

Slung across his shoulder is the little girl. Her body is limp. I can't tell if she's dead or just passed out as a result of the overwhelming ordeal she is being put through. The monster turns towards me, almost certainly having heard the echoes of the trees I've just smashed into pieces.

I freeze, luckily just far enough away that he cannot see me. If I was a meta now, did that mean I could do anything? Am I invincible like The Governor? I'd certainly gained some type of powers by enabling these bands on my wrists but how can I possibly be sure? Sam Wilkerson thought he was invincible too. He held a pay-per-view TV special where he'd planned to survive inside of a building as it was demolished to clear the way for a new mall. They buried a casket with only an ear inside of it, because that's all they could find.

It was too big of a risk to take. I reach into my pocket and pull out my cell phone to dial 911 again.

"911. What's your emergency?"

"I need help. I called earlier and no one came. I'm in the forest near mile marker forty-two on Old Brooksville Highway and there's a little girl in danger. There's a man with a knife and he's going to kill her. He already sta..."

I stop myself from telling her the truth. If I was stabbed last night by this man, how could I explain to her that I'm perfectly fine now? Can't risk it.

"Sir, is this a prank call?" she asks.

"What? No! Absolutely not! This girl is in danger!"

"Sir, we have a unit at the location you reported to us and they have not found anything. This is a serious investigation sir and if you are wasting police resources, you are breaking the law," she tells me.

"I'm not lying to you! Look, can't you track my phone or something?" I ask.

"If you're just going to turn your phone off again sir, this conversation is pointless."

"I didn't! Look, my phone is on right now. You think I'm lying to you and breaking the law? Fine, come and arrest me."

I place the phone down on a rock, making sure not to accidentally hang up. This should lead them right to me. Regardless of what happens now, I need to save this little girl. I'm not sure why, or how I was given a second chance but I was. And I need to take it. I run towards the man and his young victim, stopping just a few feet behind him.

"Put her down and get away from her!" I yell towards the man.

He looks back at me, wide eyed. The sound of my voice makes him jump. He clearly wasn't expecting company out here.

He is a pale, thin man. Wiry frame. Thick glasses magnify his eyes to the point where they seem to take up half the real estate on his face. His hair is greasy and slicked to the top of his head in a severe part. The white, old button-down shirt he wears has yellow stains under each arm the color of urine. In his back pocket is the knife he used to stab me in the back, still stained red with my blood.

"That's right. I'm not dead. Nice try though," I yell towards him.

He looks at me for a long moment. Then at the girl slung over his shoulder. He drops her to the ground, and I'm relieved to hear her cry out when she hits the ground. The pink flower patterned dress she's wearing is caked in dirt and torn, but she's still alive.

"Now step away from her..," I begin to say before I notice him reaching into his back pocket. The pocket holding the blood stained butcher knife. I yell to him to stop, but it's no use. He already has the knife held high above his head as he turns towards the little girl. The knife begins its fall, towards the barely conscious little girl's chest, as he put the entire weight of his body behind it.

That's when time seems to stop. The man's arm hangs there in the air. I do not even realize that my feet seem to have started moving without my consciously giving them the order to do so. Again, the world has slowed down around me as I rush through the trees. I feel nothing but anger. Anger at this man, this monster, who derives satisfaction from killing the most innocent. A man who receives pleasure from their torture. This monster who tried as hard as he could last night to end my life. To crush my brother's world so he would have to bury the third, and last, member of his family.

I don't throw a punch, like you would expect I would. Like a hero would. I honestly just don't know how to punch. Even if I did, it wouldn't have come as second nature quickly enough in that moment. Instead, I do what any kid on the playground who doesn't really want to fight, or doesn't know how to, would. I push him.

The difference here though as opposed to the schoolyard is that when I push him, he doesn't get a chance to push back. He flies about three hundred feet backwards through the woods instead. Bouncing between trees like a pinball. In retrospect, a punch probably would have been much more humane.

I stand for what seems like an eternity, desperately trying to catch my breath. It's not the running, or the shove, that has me out of breath. It's the adrenaline coursing through my veins at the idea that this little girl almost died. And that I almost certainly just killed a man. Finally, I snap back into the real world and catch eyes with the frightened little girl. I pull the dirty rag out of her mouth.

"Everything's going to be alright now, okay?" I say.

She nods, but is still trembling with fear.

The knots are even tighter than they were before. I start fumbling with them again but have the same amount of luck. It occurs to me that I could use the same strength that just rocketed a man through a dozen trees to pull the ropes loose, but I'm afraid of to. What if I pull the wrong rope and inadvertently suffocate this poor girl?

"What's your name?" I ask, trying desperately to keep the girl's mind off of what just happened until I can get her free.

"M...m...egan," she stutters.

"It's nice to meet you Megan. We're gonna get you out of here," I say.

I hear footsteps crunching leaves in the distance. Dogs barking. Authoritative shouts from men in the distance. It's the police. They've traced my phone. I need to get out of here. There's no way I can explain how I did all of this without revealing the truth. I don't even understand how I got these metabands, so how could I possibly explain it to them? What if they throw me in jail? What if I'm interrogated? Metas are supposed to be extinct. They might not be thrilled that at least one of them is back.

I wipe the tears from the girl's cheeks.

"I'm sorry. I have to go. The police are here now. They'll take care of you. Everything is going to be alright," I tell Megan.

"What the hell is this!?" I hear a police officer scream.

They must have found the tangled corpse of the man. I turn and the entire world grinds to a halt once again. It's time to get out of here, and within what must have been seconds, I'm home.

FIVE

"Connor?" Derrick asks from the living room.

I wake up in my bedroom. It seems like only seconds ago I was in the forest. I'm not exactly sure how I even got here. I look behind me, half expecting to see a cartoon-style cutout of my silhouette in the wall. Luckily there is none, but then how did I get in here? Can I teleport? Walk through walls?

"Connor?" His footsteps are coming towards my room.

I can't tell if I've been asleep for ten seconds or ten hours. A glance over towards the window and the sunshine streaming into my bedroom confirms that it's more likely the latter. I look down at my arms and see that I'm still wearing the metabands. That might cause some suspicion. Oh, and I'm also floating about a six feet over my bed. Dammit.

"Are you in there?" Derrick asks from the other side of the door.

Shit. This is not going to be easy to explain to anyone, let alone a conspiracy nut like Derrick. I have to get these things off of me, but they won't budge an inch. How do you turn these things off? Think. I must have watched a million metahuman videos online. Two million, if you include the really crazy ones that Derrick's shoved down my throat over the years. What I never saw in any of these was how to actually turn these damn things off. Surely there must be a way. Most of the metas were suspected to have had secret identities. Day jobs. 'Normal' lives. That's when I realize I am over thinking all of this.

How do you turn a computer on? Hit the power button. How do you turn a computer off? Hit the power button. How do you turn metabands on? Click them together. How do you turn meta bracelets off? Bingo.

I collapse onto my bed just as Derrick turns the doorknob and walks into my room. The metabands are tucked under the sleeves of my sweatshirt, and Derrick doesn't seem to notice them. Either that or he's too mad to.

"Where in the hell were you!?" He's pissed.

"I was here. In bed."

"Here!? No you weren't. You were gone all night! No one could find you. The cops-"

"Cops!?"

"Yes genius. The cops. The ones you called to report the insane kidnapper that you ran into in the woods? Remember? They've been looking all over for you."

"Oh my God," I say out loud. I hadn't even thought about how I would explain all of this. Granted, when I called 911, I didn't expect to become a metahuman soon afterwards and be able to take care of the situation myself.

"So?" Derrick asks.

"I don't know," I tell him. At least that's kinda the truth. I actually don't know.

"You don't know? You're at the center of one of the biggest stories in the last decade and you 'don't know'? How the hell did you even get in here past all of the reporters?" Derrick asks.

"Reporters?" I ask.

"Yes, reporters. The one's who have been on the front lawn for the last hour demanding to speak with you, so you can tell them all about the world's first metahuman that anyone's seen in almost ten years."

Oh no. I haven't even had these metabands for a full day yet and already my "secret" identity is blown. It's not my fault; I'm new at this. I should get a do-over, but I somehow doubt that option is on the table. Wait. Maybe these are the type of bands that some fringe theorists suspected allowed for some type of limited time travel into the past? Nah, I'm never that lucky.

"Hello?" Derrick says.

Oh. Right. I was talking with him. Got lost in my own mind.

"So?" he asks.

"I don't know what to say, Derrick. I can't lie to you. It's true," I say.

What choice do I have at this point? He's caught me red handed. Lying isn't an option any more. Even though he's my own brother, I would not be able to trust him with a secret this big. It's too dangerous for him to know. Hell, I can't even trust myself with a secret this big. He'll try his best to keep it a secret, I know he will, but eventually he'll slip. It'll be an accident of course, but that doesn't mean everything won't change. The first metahuman in ten years? Something tells me that the government will be more than a little interested in talking with me. Keeping me in a cell. Dismantling the world's only working metabands, even if that means cutting my arms off to get to them.

"So what did he look like?" Derrick asks.

There's no use in lying, so I tell him the truth.

"He was disgusting. Sweaty and dirty. Greasy hair and thick glasses. He looked exactly like what you would think someone capable of that would look like," I tell him.

"What? No! Not the pervert, I don't care what he looked like. No. What did the meta look like?" he asks me.

"The what?" I reply confused.

"The meta! The meta that saved the kid, and not to mention your ass, obviously. What did he look like? Was he here? Is that how you got in here undetected?! Oh my God, I can't believe this. An actual real-life meta! This is insane!" Derrick practically screams.

"So you're not mad at me?" I ask.

"I'm furious at you, but I'll deal with that later. What did he look like? Was he wearing a suit. Wait! Was it a she?! What powers did they have? Obviously they can teleport, that's how you got here. And they must have some type of super strength based on the number of pieces they found that pervert in."

He's pacing around my room. I've never seen him so excited.

"I'm going to go let the reporters know that you're here. They cannot *wait* to talk to you," Derrick says as he leaves the room.

I feel the back of my shirt and it feels dirt-crusted. I grab it and twist my torso to look at what it is. Oh, right. It's about a gallon of my own dried blood. Almost forgot about that. The whole 'almost dying' thing. I peel the sweatshirt off and throw my shirt under my bed. I'll deal with it later, I'm certainly not going to try to explain it now. After fishing through my dresser, I find a clean shirt and quickly throw it on.

As much as I was not prepared for the experience I had in the woods the night before, I am even less prepared for what greets me as I step out my front door. There must be at least a hundred reporters from all around the world. Satellite trucks line the street outside for at least two blocks in either direction. Some of the news organizations have even built scaffolding, just so their camera crews could get a shot of my house over the absolute sea of people crowded outside. Even though it's still early morning, I'm blinded by the lights attached to all of their cameras. Microphones are thrust into my face as my eyes struggle to adjust to the daylight and flashing bulbs.

"Mr. Connolly. Can you tell us what the meta that saved the young girl looked like?" Shouts an unseen reporter, somewhere in the mass.

"Uhh, I'm not really sure. It was pretty dark out."

"Mr. Connolly! Do you consider yourself a hero for standing up to that monster in an attempt to save the little girl before the metahuman arrived?"

"Oh, uh, no. The meta was definitely the hero. I just called the police."

"Connor. Is it true that this new meta considers you his human sidekick now?"

"What? Uh, no. I mean, I have no idea."

Sidekick? I almost laugh with relief but manage to stifle it.

I'm having an amazing run of good luck, well, aside from the whole almost getting killed thing.

"When can we expect the meta to return? Do you have the ability to contact him whenever you want?"

"No. I mean, I'm not sure. I'm sorry, I'm very tired."

"No more questions everyone, thanks," Derrick tells the disappointed reporters as he pushes me back into the house and slams the door behind us. I can still hear the reporters trying to shout their questions through the wood.

"Wow. Good job out there," Derrick tells me.

"Really?"

"No, of course not really. You sounded like you barely spoke English."

"Well sorry. Maybe it'd be easier for me if I hadn't spent all night in the woods thinking I was going to die."

"What are you talking about? By the time the cops got there, you were long gone. Where were you all night anyway?"

"I don't remember."

"What do you mean you don't remember? You saw the first metahuman anyone's seen in a decade, and you can't remember any of it? The most important thing in the world happened last night and you were there, but you can't remember any of it?"

"I need to go to sleep. I'm tired," I say. I don't know how I'm still so tired, but I'm guessing the overwhelming nature of the previous night's events probably have at least a little bit to do with it.

"Fine."

Derrick storms off into the kitchen. I don't understand why he is so mad at me. I assume part of it was some type of jealousy that it happened to me and not him. 'If he knew the half of it' I think to myself as my head hits the pillow.

Six

I sleep all day. It isn't until around eight o'clock that night that I awake from my dreamless sleep. It feels as though no time had passed at all again. The constant hum of activity that had been outside my window all day is gone. The house is quiet once more.

I sit up and enjoy it. In that moment I wonder if everything that had happened was real. The man in the woods. The metabands. His death at my hands. It takes a few moments for my brain to reboot from sleep and slowly bring these events back to the forefront of my mind.

Reaching under my bed sheets removes any of my remaining doubts. There are the metabands, still wrapped around my wrists. I pull them out from under the sheets for a moment and examine them. They are so plain. So ordinary. Dull metal that weighs almost nothing in my hands. Yet these are the most amazing devices the world has ever known.

No one knows where they actually came from. My brother is a big proponent of the "intergalactic missing shipment" theory. As in these bands came from an advanced alien civilization and were bound for another planet, perhaps a new one they had colonized. Somehow this particular package fell off the back of the intergalactic truck and crash landed onto Earth. That explains why they seemingly were all found around the same time, all those years ago: they were all a part of the same missing shipment.

There are arguments about what these supposed aliens actually used the bands for. Some claim that they were used the same way we use them here on Earth: to gain incredible abilities. Maybe they were used by the police. Or maybe they were used in war.

Another theory was that the bands weren't used to give super powers to their original designers at all. That they were designed to aid an especially weak species. Or to give them some type of other ability. But like how certain medications can have different affects on different people, these bands gave lowly humans, a species they were never designed to work with, superhuman abilities.

Regardless of what theory you subscribe to personally, no one has any idea how they actually work. Everyone's bands seemed to work differently, or at least every person seems to gain somewhat unique powers from their own personal bands. If these unique powers lie in the bands themselves or in the person using it, no one knows. And we'll likely never know, because once a set of bands has been used, they never work for another person again.

I slip the bands off my wrists and put them under my bed for somewhat safekeeping. They come off remarkably easily, at least when you consider that they are considered literally impossible to remove when they are actually powered on.

In the living room, I find Derrick transfixed to the television. One of those 24-hour news channels is on. Ten years back, there were entire channels devoted just to news concerning meta activity, good and bad. Mostly the bad though. That's what got eyeballs. Most have gone off the air now. One or two still exist to show "classic" meta footage.

They're not showing old footage today, though. What's on the screen right now is in full HD and definitely recent; and it means that I'm not alone.

"Is that her?" Derrick asks me.

On the screen is a woman, covered head to toe in a tight black and purple suit that covers her entire body, leaving only her head uncovered. Her eyes are emitting a soft white glow, obscuring most of her facial features from this distance. Her hair is blond and long, flowing in the wind one hundred feet above the city where she is flying. We both watch as she darts in and out of a building on fire. Each time she comes out of the building, another person (or sometimes two) are in her arms. She brings them down to the ground slowly before bursting back into the building for another round.

"Definitely not," I say, my jaw hanging to the floor.

Derrick slowly turns his head around towards me. His eyes wide.

"So, you mean, there are two of them?"

"I guess so. That's definitely not the one who saved me." That much isn't lying. She's not the one who saved me. I'm the one who saved me. I need to find this woman, because whoever she is, she's got this whole metaband thing figured out a hell of a lot more than I do. Now there was just the question of how to deal with Derrick.

Somehow, I was able to get into my room without breaking through the wall while I was wearing my meta bands. What I don't know is how to actually control them. Maybe I'd put them back on and be able to simply walk through my bedroom wall? But then again, maybe I'd put them on and go rocketing through the ceiling. There's no way to know for sure.

The way I see it; there are two options. The first is; I could pretend I am going to sleep and sneak out the window. This was definitely doable; I'd done it plenty of times before. The difference tonight is that if Derrick comes into my room in the middle of the night and I'm missing, he's almost certainly going to call the police. I'd just made my television debut as the "human sidekick" to the first meta seen in a very long time. Who knows what types of nutjobs could be out there looking to kidnap a person like that.

The other option is to tell Derrick that I am going out. He'd never let me, for the same reasons I just described: it's too risky for me to be out alone right now. I'd surely get a lecture all about how close I came to death last night, and how there will be people out there trying to find this meta, and that I'd make for pretty good bait.

I have to go though. If he tries to stop me, I won't let him. I don't care what he does. If it comes down to it, I'd just tell him. Tell him that I have metabands. That I'm now a meta. It'd be a gigantic risk, not only to my own well-being but also his. Ultimately though, I don't have a choice. If he tries to stop me, I have to do whatever it takes to leave, even if that means telling him the truth.

"Derrick. I'm going out," I state defiantly.

"Okay. Later," he says back, his eyes not even flinching away from the TV for a second.

Wow. That was easier than I thought. I'm halfway out the door before I realize that I haven't even brought my metabands. Not that I'm intending to use them tonight. I'm still terrified of them, but I should have them on me. Just in case. Plus, who knows what government agent could show up here tonight, maybe with a search warrant in hand, demanding that Derrick let them ransack the house.

I was lucky that poor little girl didn't realize I was the same person, she was probably too much in shock, but shock wears off. At first, they might ignore her insistence that I was the only one there, but after some time, they may begin to decide it's worth looking into. If tonight's that night, I can't take the chance.

I pull the bands out from under my bed. They're even lighter than I remember. I take a moment to look at them again. There really is nothing to them. For something so advanced and futuristic, they are exceedingly simple. You would not be able to tell the difference between these and a simple piece of aluminum. I slip one over my wrist, just to see what it's like again. It seems impossibly large around my frail little wrists and for a moment, I'm not even sure how I could keep these on without them just falling right off. Before I can complete my own thought, the band changes shape. The metal becomes almost liquid and wraps tightly around my wrist before becoming solid again. I can still move my wrist unencumbered, but now it is covered in a skintight metallic sheen. I guess that explains how they won't fall off.

I'm not worried about them falling off now, but I've got a new problem: I can't get this damn thing off. It is literally skintight, and there is no way to wedge a fingernail or anything else between it and the skin on my forearm. Why did I do this? Maybe I need to activate them before they'll deactivate? Possibly, but that's an awfully big risk. I barely remember what happened the first time I activated them. Did it make a noise? A flash of light? Did it leave a three foot crater around where I was standing? I honestly can't remember what happened because I was in such a haze. I can't risk activating them in here, unless I'm ready to explain to Derrick why half the roof got torn off.

I stuff the other band in my pocket and look around for options. There in the corner of my closet is another hoodie. It's too hot out tonight for a hoodie, unless you're going down to the water, but I've got no other choice. I can't leave the house with my arm encased in liquid metal and expect no one to notice.

When I pick up the hoodie, I notice something beneath it in a pile of clothes: a ski mask. The kind that covers your entire face except for three holes for your eyes and mouth. I'd already told myself that I wasn't going to use the bands, but it would seem that my circumstances have changed. It's at this point that I realize I'm smirking to myself, because of course it would be awesome to actually turn these things on again, regardless of how I try to convince myself otherwise. I stuff the ski mask inside one of the side pockets of the hoodie and head out.

"See ya Derrick," I say as I pass him by.

I barely get even a grunt in return. He's sitting so close to the TV that he's going to go blind. On the screen is a slow motion replay of the woman with the glowing eyes, staring right into the camera, even though she must be hundreds of feet away. The camera zooms in digitally, the type of zoom that's really just blowing up the image itself and her face becomes larger. No more clearer though. She still looks as though she's staring right at the camera. Right through it even, into my living room. Right at me. I open the screen door into the night.

As I leave I pull my phone out of my pocket and glance at it. There's three missed calls and a bunch of texts from Jim. The last of which says he saw me on TV and to call him. Sorry buddy, it's gonna have to wait tonight.

SEVEN

Finding a meta isn't as easy as it seems. Well, to be honest, I didn't really think it would be that easy. I also didn't have an idea about how to search for her. So, I just kinda found myself wandering the streets.

Bay View City has definitely seen better days. I wasn't around for those better days of course, but I know they couldn't have been much worse than this. You can still see the beautiful classic architecture underneath the facades of the newer buildings. The $0.99 Stores built over buildings that have been there for close to a hundred years with ornate fixtures on their roofs that reach high into the city sky. The dive bars inside of what used to be swanky hotels. The hotel rooms above them turned into rooms rented by the hour and crack dens.

It was beginning to look hopeless that I'd find the meta woman with the glowing eyes. I'd been wandering around for nearly three hours without even a hint of luck. I visited the now burned out building from which she saved nearly fifty people earlier tonight. Nothing.

The idea of setting up a honeypot crossed my mind. Maybe get myself into trouble and see if she appears. It was too risky though. What if she didn't show up? After all, there has to be plenty of crime happening tonight, and it's not like anyone else has seen her since the building fire. I knew, I'd spent the night with one earbud in, listening into the police scanner through an app on my phone. A little bit easier than the old days I imagine.

If I did set up a honeypot and she didn't show, I thought I might be able to fall back on my metabands. But that was still too risky. Firstly, I had no guarantee that the metabands would even work when I needed them to. Secondly, I had no intention of accidentally killing someone, who was just trying to mug me for the fourteen dollars in my wallet, in case the trap I set didn't work.

That was when I remembered last night. That I killed a man. Sure, you could say that he deserved it. According to the news, this wasn't his first offense. Walter Houser. A convicted child molester, rapist and murderer. Sentenced to forty-three years in federal prison only to have his sentence reduced to twelve due to overcrowding. Overcrowding in the prisons became a big problem during the metahuman rising. Metas were able to round up criminals better than any law enforcement agency ever could, and combined with the media attention and the general public's wanting to perceive these new metas as our saviors, meant that conviction rates had never been higher.

He deserved to die, but did I deserve to be the one who killed him? A monster like that could never be reformed. That much was certain. But that didn't mean that I had the right to be his executioner. A lot of the old metahumans killed. It was part of who they were, but some had chosen not to. It was an attempt on their part at setting a positive example for the rest of society. Showing them that just because they had powers, didn't mean that suddenly they were gods.

Metas did occasionally screw up. When they did, the same media that had vaulted them into fame and stardom turned on them quickly. The most famous of which of course was the case of The Magician. The public loved him and he could do no wrong. While he wasn't necessarily one of the most powerful or famous metas, he made up for what he lacked in abilities with his charm. In a world where most metas were considered to take themselves way too seriously, The Magician was always quick with a joke and willing to appear on morning talk shows, late night shows, etc. His power was relatively simple: he could make things disappear. Just about anything really, there weren't limits, it seemed. Where they went, no one knew, not even The Magician himself. While this might not sound like an especially amazing ability to have, it came in handy more than once.

The Magician was famous for appearing just in the nick of time during a tense situation, maybe a kidnapping or police stand-off, and immediately diffusing the situation by making the weapon involved disappear. A gunman becomes much less of a threat when his gun simply disappears from his hands. Or so one would think.

There was an especially tense and high profile stand-off that The Magician was called in for by the police. It was outside the home of a famous actress, Lauren Richards. Beautiful and talented, it was rare for a summer to go by without a new blockbuster movie starring Lauren Richards. She was even known to have dated a couple of metas. Of course these relationships never lasted very long. I can't imagine how a relationship could when both people involved are essentially living double lives.

The situation was about as routine as these things got for The Magician. All he had to do was find his way down to the police barricades, a feat easy for him since he could make himself disappear and reappear wherever he pleased, focus on the weapon and make it disappear. From there, the police would just storm the stunned gunman and take him into custody.

The Magician arrived unbeknownst to the crazed stalker and crouched behind a squad car to focus on the gun. He had it within his sights and put the first and middle finger of each hand to his temples to focus on the gun and make it disappear. This is when Starlight, one of Ms. Richards's former "friends" appeared in the sky and yelled, "Let her go!"

No one had expected Starlight to appear out of nowhere, so understandably everyone was startled. Unfortunately that included The Magician. His gaze and focus shifted in the split second he had intended to make the gun disappear. Only a foot to the right, but it was enough. Lauren Richards was a foot to the right, and in an instant she was gone. The stalker's gun went off but only shot empty space. He stood stunned, as did the police, before eventually rushing in to grab him.

The Magician didn't move either, and Starlight swooped on top of him in a blind rage, drilling him into the concrete. He demanded that The Magician bring her back. That he make her reappear.

The court case carried on for almost a year. 'Where did Lauren Richards disappear to?' was the question on everyone's mind.

When The Magician appeared on television, or at public events, he had a standard catch phrase whenever anyone asked where the object he had just made vanish went: "A magician never reveals his secrets." Now he was on trial in front of the entire world, pleading with them to believe that he did not actually know where the things he made vanish went. That it wasn't a secret. And that if he could bring back Lauren Richards, he would.

The media turned on him hard. Gone was the charming, affable everyman hero that the public could identify with. In his place was a vain monster of a man who made a woman the entire world loved disappear to a place he wouldn't reveal out of misplaced pride. A verdict was reached and The Magician was incarcerated for life.

Incarceration is an interesting thing when you're a meta. Obliviously, it's not like they can just throw you in a regular prison and expect that you won't use your powers to escape. That's why Silver Island was created. A special maximum security prison just for metas that had turned bad and refused to power down their metabands to surrender them. There were always at least two "good" metas on rotation at any given time. Part of their penance to the government for protecting their secret identities. Luckily for them, The Magician did not possess any type of extraordinary strength among his abilities, but his ability to teleport made for an interesting problem for the prison scientists to solve. Their solution was a type of metal mesh Faraday cage from which The Magician could never leave. It kept his abilities grounded to within that cage itself. He could still make himself disappear and reappear, but he was always confined to his cage.

I don't think I'll suffer the same fate as The Magician. Luckily the man I killed wasn't the type of person society cares about receiving a fair trial. But still. I'll always know that I killed him. Whether he deserved it or not isn't the question. The question is; whether or not I had the right to carry out his punishment.

It was near midnight now and still absolutely no sign of the woman with the glowing eyes. I could turn around and go home. That would be the smart option. After all, I'm in no rush. But still. I need to know who she was. I want her help. I have to try something.

I found a nearby fire escape that had its ground floor ladder broken loose. I jumped up to grab it and down it came. Counting the floors with my finger, it looked like an even dozen. Not exactly a skyscraper but certainly high enough for me to get a good enough vantage point, and more importantly, for the rest of the city to not have a good vantage point of me.

I quickly discover a dozen floors is more than you think when you have to climb them the old fashioned way. It's even more than that when the stairs are rust covered metal, and a wrong step will send you careening down to the concrete below.

Upon reaching the roof, I pause for a moment to take in the city. A distant police siren wails. Listening in on my police scanner app, I already know that it's just a minor traffic accident over on Franklin Street. I look down at my right wrist again and pull up the sleeve of my hoodie. The metaband was still there, attached to me like a second skin. Reaching into my left pocket, I pull out the other one and place it around my left wrist. Sure enough, just like the other, it melts before my eyes and encases my wrist.

Already the strange tingling sensation is working it's way through my body. Not as powerfully as last night, but I could still feel a difference. It feels amazing. The dull pain in my right knee, where I had hit it up against part of the fire escape, instantly vanishes. The slight headache I had earlier tonight disappears.

But will this work? Would activating the meta bands somehow alert the woman with the glowing eyes to my presence? Can these things feel each other, I wonder? Would I be able to control it this time? Being a dozen floors up wasn't quite as safe as being in the middle of a forest with no one around for miles. I'm as frightened for my own safety as I am for the people down below. The metabands might protect me from a high fall, although I'm definitely not entirely sure at this point yet, but I know for a fact that they won't do a whole hell of a lot for anyone that I might happen to land on.

I'd thought about it enough though. If I was going to do this, it was now or never. I can either activate these bands and hope for the best, or go home and try again tomorrow. Trying again tomorrow wasn't much of an option though, unless I wanted to wear a hoodie all day to cover up the two metabands firmly attached to my wrists. That wouldn't be so easy to explain, considering the forecast for tomorrow was about ninety degrees. No, if I was going to try this, it had to be tonight.

The ski mask comes out of my pocket and I place it over my head. Already I'm starting to feel extremely hot in the early June heat. I look down at my wrists. Even somewhat dormant, the metabands look alien. Like they shouldn't exist. Metal shouldn't be able to move this way. One last look and a deep breath. I pull my arms towards each other in front of my chest, and smash the two metabands into each other. The sound seems to echo throughout the city as I feel energy surge through my body.

Then nothing. Not even hovering above the ground this time. I'm just standing there. Looking the same as I had. Feeling great, but no other change. Scanning the city's skyline, I look for the woman with the glowing eyes. My eyesight is phenomenal. I've always had relatively good eyesight, never needed glasses, but this was different. Everything looks like it's gone from black and white to high definition color.

But still, nothing. I can see the entire city it feels like, but if the woman with the glowing eyes is in it, or at least flying above it, I certainly can't find her. I give it another fifteen minutes or so, before I start to feel nervous. What if I can't get these damn things back off of my wrists again? Hitting them together worked before, but maybe that was a fluke. It seemed like all the metas from before were able to turn off their powers somewhat at will, but that part never seemed quite clear. Probably because very few metas were stupid enough to ever power down their bands in front of prying eyes.

"Power down," I say out loud, to no one in particular, other than the metal wrapped around my wrists.

Of course that does absolutely nothing, so I stretch my arms out again, pause for a moment, then bring them flying back towards my chest. They met with a much quieter clang now, and I feel the energy leave my body. Whew, at least I figured out for certain one part of how they work, and the most important part at that: turning them on and off. I breathe a small sigh of relief.

That is when a hand grabs my shoulder and spins me around on my feet. Before I'm even fully turned around, I feel a searing pain from my nose and my eyes begin filling with tears. My mouth feels wet too, but the wetness is coming from my nose, which is now gushing with the blood. I reach up to feel my face when I feel pressure on my arms that stops them for rising towards my face. I can vaguely feel the cool metallic bracelets that had been on my wrists slide down my hands. I don't understand what is happening, but in that moment, all I care about is the excruciating pain emanating from my face.

Finally I'm able to grab part of my hoodie and wipe away the tears from my eyes enough so that I can see who or what is in front of me. The figure of a man stands before me, but he's covered almost entirely in darkness. The only exception is the two white spots floating about six feet in the air, right where the eyes would be on a man who was about six foot, three inches tall. There's one other things I can see: my two metabands being held by hands covered with black gloves.

"If you're planning on learning how to use these, I suggest making a more careful observation of your surroundings before turning them off," A gruff voice says to me from the darkness.

I rip off my ski mask. It doesn't matter if this person knows who I am now. If they are going to kill me, there's nothing I can do to stop them anymore, anyway. All the mask managed to do was encumber my view even more than the tears already had. In a move of desperation, I lunge for my metabands. It might seem stupid, but whoever this is, intends me harm and getting back those bands is my only hope.

Less than an instant after I feel my muscles constrict in preparation to lunge, something heavy smashes into the left side of my face. I hear a loud noise and the left side of my face is numb. My jaw is broken. *Obliterated* might be a better word to describe it, actually. I drop to the ground, doubled over in pain. I feel the world slowly close around me for the second time in twenty-four hours and wonder if I will wake up this time.

EIGHT

Upon regaining consciousness, I've completely forgotten what has happened before. It's that feeling of waking up in a strange place, and your brain spends what feels like an eternity trying to piece together where exactly you are and how exactly you got there. The first memory that floods into my mind is back when I'm in the woods. For a long moment, I believe that is where I am now, until I think about my back and feel no pain. That is when the memories of tonight come flooding back. I was up on the roof of a building.

Looking for someone.

I can't remember who.

The meta bands were activated though, weren't they? They were. But I remember pain. Could it be that the bands didn't work?

No. I powered down the bands. Now I remember. The bands were powered down right before the pain began. The pain. My nose and jaw. Almost certainly they were broken. But now they feel... fine. I don't feel any pain at all. In fact, I feel remarkably good. My arms are outstretched again though, just like they were in the woods. I move to lift my right arm to sit upright but it won't budge.

Turning my head towards it, I can see that I have my meta band on. That explains the lack of pain. I was injured but somehow my metaband is back. That's how I've healed, and why I feel fine again. I strain to move my right arm but nothing. That's strange. These bands felt heavy the first time I lifted them, but they've never felt heavy since. I turn to my left side and try to move that arm. Nothing. Absolutely nothing.

That is when I notice a second metal band. A band that seems like it's part of the metal table I'm on. Why am I laying on a metal table? And why is it almost pitch black in here? With that thought, almost as if on cue, I hear a click above me and a whirring electrical sound, right before I'm blinded by light from above.

My eyes are squinting as tight as they can be but it's no use, I'm still blinded. A feeling of horror comes over me as I realize what's happened: they found me. The government. I'm in some lab, tied down. Completely in the dark, while they prepare to figure out how these metabands really work. Or to run *tests* on me and see what my weaknesses are. It makes sense. Somehow, they were following me all night and waiting for their one opportunity. The one moment I was vulnerable, and they seized it.

So here I am. Alive, but completely defenseless. If my metabands were activated, I could leave this table without any problem. I could just rip these other metal bands holding me down right out from the table itself. But they're not activated. And while I'm strapped down here, I may as well not be wearing them at all, because there's absolutely no way to turn them on in this position. Now I wait. Because there's nothing else that I can do.

Suddenly, I can feel eyes on me. They've been there the whole time. Someone is standing beside me. I can't see them but I can sense their presence. Considering my condition, it's hard to believe that they would be friend rather than foe.

"I take it by now, you've figured out where you are," a voice says to me.

I don't respond.

"Did you not hear me?" the voice says.

"Yeah."

"And where is that?"

"A government lab."

The figure beside me laughs. At least I think it's a laugh. It sounds more like a gravely grunt, but it's still lighter in tone than any of the words that have come out of his mouth so far.

"If you were in a government lab, they would have had those metabands far away from you by now. Trust me."

"How am I supposed to trust someone who broke my nose and my jaw, so they could strap me down to a table in a dark room?"

"Good point, but not my concern. Where did you find those?" he asks, presumably referring to the metabands and not the new sneakers I happen to be wearing. The voice is now coming from a different part of the room. Whoever is speaking to me is pacing around the outside of the perimeter where the light meets the darkness.

"What does it matter to you?" I say in an act of uncharacteristic defiance. Maybe getting a few bones broken knocked something lose in me.

"Why wouldn't it matter to me?" The voice is directly in front of me now, as it steps out of the darkness and into the light from above.

I can't believe what I am seeing.

"Midnight," I say out loud.

Midnight. When the first wave of meta humans started appearing on Earth, a lot of people were frightened. You have to remember that this was before anyone, and I mean anyone, the government included, understood or knew what they were. A lot of folks thought they were aliens from another planet. Or some type of government experiment gone horribly wrong. A threat from the Russians, or the Chinese.

The first year of metahumans was almost total chaos. Miscommunication about who and what they were ran rampant. Everywhere you went, everyone had a theory or heard a story from another guy, whose brother's brother-in-law's friend works for the C.I.A., blah blah blah. You get the idea. People were afraid to leave their houses to go to work, and they were also transfixed to their televisions for any and every update.

It was around this time the vigilantes started popping up. At first it was just copycats. A guy watching TV decides being a metahuman looks like fun, so he spray paints an old wet suit and decides to hit the streets for himself to see if he can join in on the good times, even if he doesn't possess a pair of metabands. The metas that leaned towards the more villainy side of the spectrum, used to use these guys for target practice.

But then a few started popping up that could hold their own. Many came forward out of necessity. They came from neighborhoods that the police didn't have time to visit any more now that they were so busy cleaning up after the metas. Some formed alliances with the good metas, which more or less kept the bad ones off their backs and away from their neighborhoods. If something happened to them, you'd have half a dozen metas after you for it, so it just wasn't worth it for most.

The vigilantes were popular. Something for kids to aspire to. The ones that were realistic enough to know that they would never find a pair of metabands for themselves. Everything changed when Midnight appeared, though. No one had ever seen anything like him.

While most vigilantes were little more than barroom brawlers at best, Midnight was a different beast altogether. Little footage of him actually existed at the time. It got to the point that many swore he was simply an urban legend. The result of a handful of similar looking vigilantes having a good outing or two, and their stories all being combined to make one almost super human sounding vigilante named Midnight. All of that changed when he actually took down a meta though.

The meta's name was simply 'Fire'. What he lacked in originality, he made up for in mayhem and destruction. An ex-con released after serving half his sentence for multiple counts of arson and homicide, his ability was turning the oxygen in the air surrounding him into pure fire. As far as abilities go, there wasn't too much you can do with an ability like that to have a positive effect on the world. Luckily for Fire, he wasn't interested in that anyway. Fire was a psychopath through and through. What he lacked in intelligence, he more than made up for in pure evilness.

Fire's gleeful march through downtown, incinerating everything and person had been ongoing for nearly an hour when it happens. Midnight appears out of nowhere on Main Street. Right in the middle of Fire's path of destruction. And he simply waits.

Fire laughs. His actions weren't disastrous enough to draw the attention of another metahuman yet, but they were enough to bring Midnight out of hiding. Fire redirects his flames towards Midnight as he continues his march. The heat is absolutely unbearable, even for Midnight, who from the news copter's view, you could see was wearing some type of insulated armor. Fire is now bearing down on Midnight as dozens of citizens hiding in nearby buildings take the opportunity to flee. Fire's white hot flames keep getting closer and closer to Midnight, until he is all but two feet in front of him.

That's when the manhole cover behind Fire flies about twenty feet into the air. Midnight, or rather the real Midnight, reaches up from the manhole, grabs Fire's ankles and pulls as hard as he can. Fire had no time to react and falls face first into the concrete. The Midnight waiting on the street wasn't Midnight at all. It was a sophisticated suit of armor left to stand idle. A trap. No one was ever inside of it.

Seven of Fire's teeth are knocked out of his head when Midnight rolls him over, and headbutts him for good measure, and to make certain he's out for the count. Even though the police swoop in on the scene mere seconds after this transpires, all they find is Fire bound with a pair of Teflon handcuffs. Midnight has already descended back into the entrance of the sewer from where he appeared.

And now, he is standing above me. Midnight was recognizable by the fact that he has always been almost completely unrecognizable, by his own design. His entire body was covered head to toe in plated body armor. Over that there was some type of black neoprene. The only recognizable feature in the armor, was a simple dark grey crescent moon, barely visible. The only part of his body that was exposed was his jawline, a look popularized by many of the more well-known metas. Even his eyes were covered by some white lenses that made it appear as though he had no pupils, although obviously whatever material this was, it allowed Midnight to still see through it. Probably even better, since undoubtedly there was some form of enhanced goggles buried under that cowl.

"I asked you a question," Midnight says.

"Honestly, I forgot what it even was."

"Where did you get those metabands. That's the last time I'm asking," Midnight growls.

"I don't know," I say.

"Wrong answer."

"Wait!" I scream before he has a chance to do whatever it is that was the next step after breaking my jaw.

"I'm not keeping anything from you. I'm just as confused about it as you are. One minute I'm laying in the woods bleeding to death and the next, I wake up with these things around my wrists. I don't know where they came from, and I barely understand how they work. That's the truth, I promise you."

"Hmm. You're telling the truth."

"How do you know?"

Midnight taps his cowl, next to his right eye. Looks like I was right, he does have some kind of tech in there feeding him information. There must be a lie detector or something that he can use just by looking at me. Or maybe these straps keeping me tied down to the table are equipped with sensors reading my pulse rate. Or he's just bluffing. Whatever, I don't actually care right now because at least he believes me, and I won't be getting any more bones broken tonight if I'm lucky. With another tap on his wrist, the shackles holding me to the table release and I'm free.

"You really don't know how those things work yet do you?" he asks.

"No."

"You're going to get yourself killed out there then."

"You think that idea hasn't crossed my mind?"

"Watch it, kid. I'm trying to help you here."

"Yeah, I noticed that when you broke half of my face."

"That was necessary to ensure you could be taken into custody without incident. Even deactivated, the metabands healed you. I knew they would."

"Sure, and the mental scars from nearly being beaten to death will heal just fine too, I'm sure."

"Toughen up. You're a meta now. Things aren't going to get easier from here. This is the path you've chosen."

"I didn't choose anything! These bands just appeared on me."

"If you want them gone forever, I can help with that."

"Well, I mean, let's not get hasty. I haven't been a superhero for even twenty-four hours yet, let's see if it takes to me first."

"Superhero? You think some foreign technology is all it takes to make you a superhero?"

"Hey! I saved a little girl's life today, buddy."

"And you killed a man in the process."

"I'm not proud of that, but it's not like he was an innocent bystander. He was a monster."

"That's not for you to decide."

"Well, what's done is done. I can't change what happened and what I did."

"But you can make sure it never happens again."

"Oh yeah? How's that?"

"By learning how to control yourself and those bands."

"And how am I going to do that?"

"Well are you afraid of them?"

"Yes."

"Then that's the first problem."

NINE

Hovering is harder than it looks. The metabands naturally want to shoot you into the atmosphere, as the dent I've created in Midnight's ceiling proves. At first, it was nearly impossible to even get off the ground, now it feels impossible to land. My feet dangle an inch from the ground, but I cannot relax enough to land.

Midnight tells me that flying is one of the hardest abilities to control. Now that I can *kinda* do it for myself, it's no wonder that a lot of the original metas who died, did so because they accidentally flew into a building at a thousand miles an hour, or lost their concentration at thirty thousand feet.

Midnight, of course, has never used metabands himself, but his knowledge of how they work exceeds that of anyone I've ever heard about. That includes the forum junkies that Derrick keeps me apprised of. I ask Midnight how he knows so much about the metabands, but he ignores the question entirely. I'm not surprised.

He tells me that I'm lucky. My bands seem to have some sort of built-in protection mechanism that he hasn't seen before. Most metas with super-human strength and the ability to protect and repair their bodies have to concentrate on doing so. I don't. It's like that ability is on auto-pilot. According to Midnight, my bands look identical to the first wave versions the world saw all those years ago, but there's no way to know for sure if there isn't something different about these ones. Of course, it could also just be how I'm wired, he says. There could be something about my brain, and how it interfaces with these bands, that just works. The way sometimes a person is just a natural, that might be me, at least in regards to the strength/protection ability. Certainly not flying, as the increasingly deeper dent in Midnight's ceiling attests to.

After a couple of hours of this, it's obvious that I'm not going to get it tonight. It's late and I haven't had an actual *good* night's sleep in two days now. Midnight tells me that learning to control my abilities while I'm exhausted is important. Maybe the most important. I'm nodding off as he tells me this of course. I can't stop thinking about my bed. Warm and soft. Quiet and cozy. There's literally no place on Earth that I'd rather be right now, than lying in that bed. I want to be there so badly that it starts to feel like I actually am in my bed.

Now I am in my bed. It's just as warm and cozy as I'd imagined it. I don't know how I got here, but I've never been so glad to be in it I think as I drift off to sleep.

I wake up the next morning and cannot for the life of me figure out how I got here. I remember being at Midnight's and just being so, so tired. The next thing I remember is being here. So this means I can teleport now too? If learning just how to hover seemed difficult, I can't even begin to understand how it is that I was able to teleport.

Midnight's not going to be happy about this, I have a feeling. I still don't know how to get to his headquarters, or lair, or whatever it is, since he took me there while I was knocked unconscious.

I stumble into the kitchen, where Derrick is so engrossed in whatever is on his laptop screen, that he doesn't notice he's dripping half of his cereal and milk onto the kitchen table as he shovels it into his mouth.

"Good morning," I say as I find my way to the cabinet and look for the cereal box.

Derrick barely grunts back.

"More metahuman happenings?" I ask, not even thinking about last night. What if someone saw what happened? I was careful, I had a ski mask on the whole time, but still. What if it came off when Midnight was beating me half to death and I didn't notice?

Nah. He's more careful than that. Right?

"Ehh. Nothing conclusive. Lots of people on the boards saying they saw things, but no one grabbed a picture or video? Give me a break," Derrick says.

I haven't noticed that my right hand is shaking so hard that I'm missing the bowl I'm pouring my cereal into. I don't know why this is making me so nervous. What did I expect Derrick to say? "Oh yeah, here's a picture of you flying above the city on the front page of today's newspaper, by the way..." If I'm going to do this whole secret identity thing, I've got to start getting a little bit better of a grip on my own emotions.

"Heh, yeah. Sounds like they've got too much time on their hands. Speaking of which, are you working from home today? I thought you'd said there was a meeting you had to go in for?" I ask Derrick.

"Crap!" he exclaims. "I'm late!" Derrick grabs another mouthful of cereal, again most of it doesn't make it to his mouth, as he stands up and grabs his bag. He's out the door before I'm able to say bye. The door slams and there is nothing but quiet inside the house.

I'm alone. Finally. I walk back into my bedroom and find my metabands. I sit with them for a long time and just hold them in my hands. They weigh almost nothing yet are indestructible. A mystery that even the brightest scientists in the world could never solve. Granted, there were many more mysteries to the bands that they were focusing their energies on trying to figure out, rather than just the mystery of why they were so light.

My mind begins to wander. I think about how I used the bands to save that little girl from that monster. He might not have had powers and abilities, but in those woods, it didn't matter. It didn't matter, that is, until these bands appeared on my wrists out of nowhere. If they hadn't, I certainly would have died that night, and so would she. This is the first time the weight of the situation is fully being digested, but it's not long before my brain moves onto darker places. Like the idea that things may have happened differently if I had these bands the day my parents died. Obviously not much would have been different if I had these when I was so young, but what if that happened to them happened today? Would I be able to save them?

Work! I completely forgot. A few weeks ago, I'd interviewed for and received a summer job at the local Electrotown. Today was, no *is*, supposed to be my first day. I look at the clock. It's 9:48. My training shift starts at 10. Dammit. I don't remember very much from what they explained to me about the job, honestly it seemed like any idiot could do it, but I do remember one thing: they did not care for tardiness. There's some type of point system, and that's about as far as I had listened. I'm always surprisingly punctual, so I didn't imagine this part of the job description would really matter to me. Of course, what I didn't imagine at the time, was that I'd be in possession of metabands, which would kinda throw my life for a little bit of a loop this week.

Twelve minutes to make it to Electrotown. There's no way I can make it in time. Being late on the first day is almost certainly the type of thing they'll frown upon enough to just tell me to forget about coming back tomorrow. I really need this job. While me and Derrick received a little bit of money from the government after our parents' deaths, that will end once I reach eighteen. I need to start pulling my own weight if I want anything other than peanut butter and jelly sandwiches at every meal. I can't be late, but no bus on Earth is going to get me there in the next twelve minutes.

Then it hits me: there are other ways to get there besides taking the bus. I look back down at the metabands lying in my hands. I don't quite understand how to control them yet, but they'd already teleported me at least twice: once back to my room after finding them and again last night at Midnight's base. I seem to be able to somewhat reliably control the ability to get me *back* to my room, but what about somewhere else?

It seems risky but what is the worst thing that could happen? Well I could teleport myself into a wall I guess. Or accidentally teleport myself a mile *above* Electrotown and enjoy the rest of my trip there, hurdling back towards the Earth.

Now that I give it more thought, I guess the worst that could happen was actually pretty terrible. I have to risk it though. I mean, I don't, but I feel like I do. I need to have a healthy amount of respect for my new powers, but right now, all I feel for them is fear. Fear will be my undoing. If I am ever going to start getting a grip on these powers, I need to start getting used to them.

Ten

The first thought that crosses my mind after I've arrived is: "Why does my foot feel wet?" I look down and find my answer: because it's in a toilet. At least the person before me had the decency to flush.

I'm in a handicap stall inside a Men's Room. Or at least I hope to God it's a Men's Room or else I've got two problems. I recognize it as the rest room inside the Electrotown that hired me (I was a little nervous before the interview and became intimately familiar with the facilities.) I pull my foot out of the toilet and shake it off then pull my phone out of my pocket to check the time. 9:52. I made it.

The relief is only temporary though, as I realize now that I need to find a way to hide my metabands. I don't have a bag with me because that would have been smart. I look all over as I power down the bands and slip them off my wrists before realizing the answer is above me. The bathroom's drop ceiling.

Back in the handicap stall, I stand on top of, rather than in, the toilet and push the ceiling tile up. It moves with ease and I'm able to pop my metabands up there for safe keeping. This is stupid, but I have no other choice. There's no other place to hide them. Tomorrow, I'll be certain to bring my bag.

After spending about four minutes precariously balancing on one leg under the hand dryer while trying to dry off my toilet water soaked right foot, it's time to give up and meet up with the assistant store manager. I tried my best but at this point, I'm going to be late anyway if I don't hurry.

Stepping out of the bathroom, I see the back of Gary, one of the managers, waiting for me. He's checking his watch and doesn't look happy.

"Hi Gary," I say. This startles him as he wasn't expecting me to come up behind him since he's facing the main entrance of the store, waiting for me.

"Connolly! You're late."

"Sorry Gary, I went to the back of the store first, thinking you might be there. I was here on time, I promise."

"Fine. Sheila called in sick today so it looks like your training is going to have to wait. You're on inventory duty."

"What's that?"

"You go in the back, and you count. And when you're done counting, you count again," Gary tells me.

Sounds like a blast. In less than twelve hours, I've gone from learning how to save the world to mindlessly counting video games over and over to make sure none have been stolen. Truth be told, I kinda enjoy the mindless task. It gives me an opportunity to finally slow down and begin to process what's been going on.

These bands are tied to me for life now. No matter what happens, they'll never work for anyone else. I can't stop thinking about the permanence of it all, and how much different my life is going to be from how I thought it would be. This line of thinking is what keeps causing me to lose track of the games that I'm supposed to be counting.

I finally manage to keep track of a count higher than a hundred when I heard a loud bang and a scream. My stomach drops. I'm not sure what had happened, but my blood turns to ice in my veins. This isn't good.

I'm all alone in the back stockroom, frozen in fear. Afraid of what I'm going to find on the other side of the door to the main sales floor. After what feels like an eternity, I walk slowly towards the stockroom door and peer out.

A man, with a black mask covering his face, has his left arm tightly around the neck of a young woman, a customer. In his right hand is a silver handgun pressed up against her right temple. She's crying. The rest of the store's customers and employees are kneeling on the ground, their hands over their heads.

"Don't anyone move, do you hear me!" the man shouts.

"Who's in charge here?"

Gary slowly raises his hand. He's a few rows back from the others.

"I am."

"Get up!" The robber yells.

Gary rises.

"Yes, of course. I'll do anything you say. Please, just don't hurt anyone. I'll go to the back and open the safe for you."

"What do you think I'm stupid? A big chain like this doesn't let some pathetic, minimum wage manager open the safe whenever he wants. That thing's on a timer and I know that. What I also know is that there's probably a silent alarm back there that you were planning to trip, wasn't there, smart guy?" the robber says with a sneer.

"No, no. Of course not. Look. I just want everyone to get out of here safely."

"Good. Then you can start by opening the cash registers and emptying everything in them into a bag."

"Okay."

The robber gestures towards the registers and Gary begins moving. He takes his employee swipe card and uses it at each register to open their cash drawers. With twenty-six registers, this is going to take a little while.

That's when I remember my metabands. They're still in the bathroom, hidden above the ceiling tiles. Is it worth the risk? Is it worth risking my life, and the lives of everyone here to get them when all this man wants is money?

But what if he doesn't want just money? What if he wants to send a message? What if the police arrive and there's a siege? What if innocent people die because I was too scared to sneak into the bathroom and end this myself? I might not have full control over my powers yet, but I'm certain I can use them to at least move quickly enough to disarm the robber before he's even aware it's happened. That much, I am sure of.

I have to risk it.

The men's restroom, where I've hidden my metabands, is less than one hundred feet away. There are store displays with laptops on top of them along the way, mostly obscuring the line of sight between myself and the robber. I can make it.

I gently push the door and it swings open, silently. I'm crouching down on my hands and knees, moving very slowly and deliberately, making certain not to make a sound. I can feel my ears are hot and can hear my own heartbeat. Fifty feet. I'm almost there. I can see the door. All I can see is the door. All I care about in the world is just making it to that door. I care about the door so much, that I don't notice the robber is next to me until I hear him pull back the hammer of the gun, which is now pointed squarely at my left temple.

"What the hell do you think you're doing?" The robber growls at me.

I can't speak. I was so close. So close to ending all of this. So close to winning. I'm barely able to stammer out, "S..s..s..sorry."

"You're goddamn right you're sorry, because now I'm going to make an example out of you."

I close my eyes for what I expect will be the last time.

A shot rings out.

I open my eyes.

I'm alive.

But Gary is not.

His body lies in-between the cash registers that the robber had ordered him to empty. His lifeless eyes stare at the ceiling as a pool of blood forms around him.

"That's what you get for trying to be a hero," the robber whispers into my ear, as he picks me up by my bright yellow Electrotown polo shirt and drags me towards the rest of the hostages.

"You see what happens when you try to show off?" he screams at the group. "You get people killed! I am not messing around here, dammit! You!" He pushes me towards

Gary's dead body. "Congrats kid. You just got a promotion. Now finish the job your old boss didn't get a chance to, and fill that bag full of money. Now!"

I stumble towards Gary in shock. Just hours earlier, this man was chastising me for being late, and now he's dead. And it's my fault. I pull the bag half filled with money out from his still warm hand. There's blood on it, and I feel sick for a moment but manage to keep it together. I can't imagine what this psychopath will do next if I do something like throw up.

Suddenly, the front doors to the store fly open so hard that they almost come off their hinges. The robber immediately grabs the woman closest to him and puts his gun up to her head. She yelps in pain at the still hot muzzle being pressed up against her bare skin.

"Back off! Back off or I start killing more people, pigs! I'm serious!" The robber yells at the doors.

That's when he walks in.

If the fact that he almost blew the doors off didn't tip you off to the fact that he was a metahuman, the head to toe blue spandex would have told you. The uniform wasn't adorned with any type of logo or symbol, something that was uncommon during the first metahuman period. The meta wore no mask either. His blond hair and blue eyes looked like they belonged to a catalog model more than a metahuman.

"Let her go," he commands the robber.

"Sure thing," the robber says as he turns the gun on the meta and fires. The shot hits his chest and he falls to the ground. In an instant, the meta is across the store, with his hand clamped tightly around the robber's throat.

"That was a silly thing to do," the meta says before casually twisting his wrist and snapping the robbers neck so loudly that half the hostages audibly gasp. Whoever this meta is, he doesn't seem big on the idea of second chances.

He walks over to Gary and places his hand on his neck to make sure he's dead. Then he walks over to me. I'm still holding the bloodied bag of money. He puts his hand on my shoulder and says, "It's all right. He won't be hurting anyone else, ever again,"

And with that, he's gone. A blue blur that flashes through the crowd of former hostages and out the front doors. The room of over a hundred employees and customers is completely silent. The moment hangs for what feels like an eternity before the SWAT team rushes in through the same front doors and brings with them the reality of the outside world.

I failed. I worse than failed. I caused a man's death. A man who did no harm to anyone. A complete innocent. This is my second murder within a week, and even though this one was not at my own hands, it feels like it was. It feels like a three hundred pound man was standing on my chest. No, not standing on it. Jumping on it. Trying to see if he could land hard enough to make my heart explode out through my yellow Electrotown polo shirt.

A member of the SWAT team pulls me outside. An EMT wraps me in one of those silver tin foil looking blanket things. I'm handed a bottle of water and brought to an ambulance. All of this is happening in slow motion. I'm stunned.

My powers didn't fail me.

I failed me.

ELEVEN

When a patrol car finally brings me home, Derrick is already there waiting. His red puffy eyes tell me that he's been crying, although I'm sure he'd never admit it. Without saying a word, he grabs me and pulls me into a hug. Derrick and I have lived alone with only each other for almost a decade now, and I think this is the first time we've actually hugged since Mom and Dad's funeral. It feels nice.

"What happened?" Derrick asks, sniffling.

"To be honest, it was all such a blur, I don't even know. A guy tried to rob the store and he shot my manager. Then some meta came in and killed him. Before anyone even knew what was going on, it seemed to be over," I tell him, somewhat honestly.

"What is happening Connor? This is the second time this week you've almost been killed and some meta has saved you. That can't be a coincidence," Derrick asks.

"I don't know what to tell you, Derrick. I'm as confused about all of this as you are," I say.

"I guess it doesn't matter. Right now, I'm just glad that you're safe. I picked up some dinner on the way home since I figured you probably haven't eaten. It's on the kitchen table if you're hungry," Derrick tells me.

"Oh. You're a lifesaver. I'm starving. Thanks."

It was true. I skipped breakfast this morning obviously since I was late and hadn't had a chance to eat anything before the... robbery. The police offered me food during my questioning, but I was too nauseous to eat then. The nausea had finally passed now though and I was absolutely starving.

Derrick retreats to his home office and laptop. The level of metahuman activity within the last few days is absolutely off the chart, and I'm sure the message boards were barely able to keep up with the speculation and cameraphone pictures of everything that has been happening lately. That is fine by me.

I could use some time alone.

I sit down at the kitchen table and pull over the bag of fast food cheeseburgers Derrick has gotten me. They are cold but I'm too grateful to complain. Unwrapping the first burger, my mouth is already salivating. I bite into it and feel something odd. Like a leaf of lettuce that is just a little too tough. I spit it out into the wrapper.

Of course.

It's a note. Folded up. I unfold it. All it reads is, "First rooftop. 01:00." There's no signature but it is pretty obvious that there were only a few people "clever" enough to sneak a note into a cheeseburger, and only one that I know personally.

TWELVE

"You know, a text message would have been just as easy," I shout into the darkness on the rooftop where I first encountered Midnight, knowing that he is already there, even if I can't see him.

"Text messages can be intercepted," a voice in the darkness says.

"Yeah, well notes stuck inside cheeseburgers can be choked on," I say back to the darkness.

"You lived," says Midnight, who is now inexplicably standing six inches behind me.

"Yeah, but it kinda ruins the rest of the burger, knowing that you've been pawing around in it leaving notes. Is that even sanitary?"

"We have more important things to discuss."

I'm starting to realize Midnight doesn't have much in the way of a sense of humor.

"The incident today wasn't your fault," he says.

"Incident? A man died. No, I'm sorry. Two men died. It wasn't just an 'incident'."

"You didn't let me finish," Midnight growls. "The incident today wasn't your fault, but the actions and decisions made, prevented you from being in a position to stop it."

"A position to stop it? I tried! I tried to get my metabands and I couldn't, okay? And that is what got Gary shot. I have to live with that now. Knowing that not only did I *not* prevent a man's death, I caused it with my stupid decisions. Are you happy now? You were right. I was wrong. I don't know what I'm doing! Okay? Happy?" I yell.

I start choking up as the words are leaving my mouth. It's hard to process all of this, and it's not until I've actually said it out loud, that it begins to hit me again. I killed Gary. I might not have pulled the trigger, but my own stupid attempt at being a hero is what set off the robber, and I will never forget that.

"Calm down," Midnight says as he puts a gloved hand on my shoulder. This is the first sign of any emotion, other than anger, I've seen from him.

"You're new at this. You did the best you could. A lot of other people would have ran out that back door, but you didn't. The robber could have just as easily shot you, and you knew that but made an attempt to get your metabands and help anyway. That's bravery. The type of bravery metabands can't give you," Midnight reassures me.

This actually does help. It doesn't fix anything, but it helps. "I just don't know what to do. I don't ever want to be responsible for anything like that ever again. This feels horrible," I tell Midnight.

"Then you won't. That's a decision you can make."

"But how?"

"There are two things. The first is: you cannot work at Electrotown."

"Don't worry. I can't imagine they'll be opening back up anytime soon after all of this."

"No. I mean you cannot work at Electrotown or any place like Electrotown. There are CCTV cameras monitoring that entire store. If I'd known you were taking a job there I would have never allowed it."

"I'm not stupid. I teleported into the restroom. Not even Electrotown has cameras in the restroom."

"And what happens when they go back to look at that security footage and notice that there's a person who comes out of the restroom that they never saw go in?"

Silence. I hadn't thought of that. I hadn't thought I'd ever need to use my powers at Electrotown, though. Or at the very least, I never thought there would be a reason for them to look at that with the security cameras.

"I didn't know what happened was going to happen," I say.

"Of course you didn't, and you never will. That's why you cannot ever, ever take these things for granted."

"Dammit. They're going to be pouring over those tapes. They're going to notice that. They already asked me way more questions than they would have because of what happened in the woods the other night. It's already so suspicious that I've been in both these places. Dammit! I'm so stupid!" I say as I begin panicking.

"Relax. It's taken care of," Midnight tells me.

"What do you mean?"

"I mean it's taken care of. The camera covering the employee entrance in the back was already out of order. I damaged the tape from the camera covering the entrance to the restroom. If anyone asks, you came in through the back that day. There's no way to prove otherwise."

This is the first bit of good news I've heard in awhile. At least since Derrick told me he got me cheeseburgers, even though they had notes stuffed inside them.

"Thank you," I tell Midnight, sincerely.

"And there are these," he says as he tosses me my metabands.

"How did you-" I manage to get out before Midnight interrupts me.

"If it was obvious to me where you would have hid these, it might have been obvious to someone else. You can't let these fall into someone else's hands. I thought I'd made that clear to you the other night but I suppose not," he says.

"Why does it matter? They're hardcoded to my DNA now anyways you said, no one else can use them," I fire back.

"And how were you planning on using them if they aren't in your possession?" he asks.

He had me there. I had felt fairly secure in the knowledge, that even if someone ever did find my metabands, there was nothing they'd be able to do with them. Hell, for all they'd know, they were just toy replicas or something. They don't do anything for anyone other than their owners, so there would be no way to tell. But if someone found these and kept them from me, that would put a pretty quick end to my career as a metahuman.

"You have to learn how to put them into sleep mode," Midnight tells me in a way that suggests the idea of putting these physical objects into a 'sleep mode' is the most obvious thing in the world. I respond accordingly with a blank stare.

"You know what sleep mode is right?" he asks. He seems like he is beginning to lose his patience again.

"Yeah, for like a computer. Not for these things," I tell him.

"Same idea. These things can go into a mode where they're somewhat inactive but still physically present."

"Meaning?"

"Meaning, for all intents and purposes, they're on you all the time but they're invisible," he explains.

"Whoa. Wait, really?" I ask.

"Well, not really. No one actually knows exactly what happens to them. The closest guess is that they temporarily shift slightly out of our reality, or dimension. They're still there, they're still present, but they're not. Do you follow?" he asks. He seems to have confused even himself.

"Not at all, but I'm willing to give anything a try. How do I do it?" I ask.

"Put them on."

I put the metabands around my wrists again. I'd almost forgotten the slight, static electric feel I get when they're on, even de-activated, as they automatically adjust themselves to wrap tightly around my wrists. It's a good feeling.

"Now just concentrate on them. Imagine that they're not there. Imagine you can see right through them to your bare arms," Midnight tells me.

I concentrate hard. Very hard.

"You're concentrating too hard. You need to relax. If you force it too hard, it won't happen," Midnight informs me.

"Oh, like a magic eye poster!" I yell excitedly and with that, the metabands around my wrists slowly fade away.

"I did it! That was awesome!" I shout.

"Good job. Now what will be more impressive, and more

important, is bringing them back," Midnight tells me, bringing me back down to Earth a little bit.

"Oh. Right. Yeah. That makes sense. Okay. Let me try," I say.

Bringing them back feels harder than making them disappear. It's easier to imagine that something isn't there than to imagine that it is. The slight panic in the back of my head, at the idea that I might never be able to bring these things back into existence, isn't helping the whole concentration thing much either.

I'm halfway through saying the words, "I can't," when the bands appear on my wrist. Like a jump cut in a film, they are just instantly there. They do not slowly materialize around my wrists, or fade in. One second there are no metabands, and the next instant, there they are, fully formed.

"Very good," Midnight says.

"How did you know I'd be able to do that?" I ask.

"It doesn't matter."

Of course it matters, but it only matters to me, so Midnight doesn't care. He doesn't care that I know almost nothing about him other than the myths passed down over the years. He doesn't care that I'm increasingly curious about how it is that he knows so much about metahumans and metabands, when he's never had them himself. Actually, he probably does care that I care about that and wishes I wouldn't. It's something he'd consider a distraction.

"Now that that problem is taken care of," Midnight begins, "we need to fix the problem of you foolishly deciding to get a job where the entire place is covered wall to wall with security cameras."

"I know. I get it. I wasn't counting on becoming a metahuman when I got my eight dollar an hour job, stocking shelves with headphones okay?" I say, losing my temper slightly.

Midnight just stares at me and says nothing.

"Okay. So what are we going to do then?" I ask to break

the silence.

"That's better," he replies.

"I need a job. Derrick's not exactly bringing in a fortune right now and once I turn eighteen, the government money stops. Not having a summer job just isn't an option, metahuman or not."

"I agree. In addition, we need you to get into better shape if you're going to be of any use to anyone."

"Better shape? What are you talking about? First off, I'm in fine shape."

"You got winded climbing the fire escape to the roof tonight."

"Oh, you saw that?"

Midnight glares at me.

"What does it matter? I've got metabands. I could become a three hundred pound couch potato and still run circles around anyone in the world. You even said yourself that my metabands were different somehow. Stronger than the others," I say.

"The metabands only multiply what you naturally are capable of," Midnight tells me.

"So I'm somewhat naturally capable of flying, and these just enhance that?" I ask sarcastically.

"No smartass. But your strength and speed are what is multiplied by the bands. And they're multiplied exponentially. So even slight improvements in your natural abilities will translate to huge improvements in your abilities when your bands are activated."

"So what does that have to do with my summer job?" I ask.

"Your summer job is at the lake. I've already made the arrangements in the city's employment database," Midnight says.

"What?! There's no way I can work as a lifeguard! Look, I know you're trying to push me to work myself harder, but I can barely swim. Me being a lifeguard is a bad idea," I plead.

"Who said anything about being a lifeguard? You're clean up crew," Midnight says.

I'm about to object to the idea of picking up garbage at the lakefront all summer and ask exactly how that's supposed to help me become a better metahuman, when the sounds of squealing tires and gunshots interrupts me.

Midnight and I lock eyes.

"Don't even think about it," he says to me before turning and leaping off the roof. Halfway to the ground, a grappling hook shoots out from the gun usually holstered to his belt. The hook grabs onto a nearby lamppost, swinging him onto the roof of the car that the gunshots came from, which is now quickly speeding away. The car rounds the corner and out of my sight.

My instincts are conflicted. Do I listen to Midnight or do I power up my metabands and finally do some good for a change? Am I ready?

One thing is for sure at least, I'm at least not waiting around to find out.

I scurry down the fire escape as quickly as possible and can still hear the car speeding away as more gunshots ring out. I'm at the bottom of the fire escape ladder when I hear the wheels squeal again and then a crash.

I run as quickly as possible down the three city blocks towards the fire. I'm almost there when the sound of another gunshot sends me ducking behind a dumpster.

Against the backlight of the fire erupting from the hood of the car now wrapped around a lamppost, I can see the silhouette of Midnight and three others. I don't know who the three others are, but they don't seem to like Midnight very much.

I stick back behind the dumpster and watch as Midnight fights the three men. His fighting is almost all counter attacks, never attacking first. He waits for one of them to throw a punch, or swing a bat before attacking himself, leveraging their own momentum to his advantage. He quickly dispatches the three men. They lay on the ground moaning as Midnight turns his back on them and begins walking back towards me.

I am in awe. He almost makes it seem too easy. Who the hell is this guy? I'd always heard tales of him, of course, the entire world has, but to see him actually fight like that? There aren't words to describe the fluidity and speed. Even metahumans can't match the grace with which he fought, I think to myself, as he casually cracks his neck, while walking down the street with the crackling of the flames behind him and the wail of sirens in the distance drawing closer.

There's something in the fire though.

Something that wasn't there before.

Something alive.

I'm not able to scream before it bursts out of the flames and throws Midnight into the nearest store window.

Good God. It is huge. A hulking, red figure that must be at least nine feet tall. Muscles bulging everywhere on its body. Whatever it is, it isn't human. And whatever it is, it is very, very pissed off.

It just caught him off guard, I tell myself. It might not be human but that hasn't stopped Midnight from winning battles before. I'm sure this will be no different, I try to reassure myself as I watch the beast stomp into the storefront it had just thrown Midnight through. A second later, Midnight comes flying through the storefront again, this time onto the street.

He begins to pick himself up when I see something come out of his mouth as he coughs. It's blood. He makes another attempt to stand before collapsing. The red beast clomps out of the busted storefront window. It looks at Midnight, sprawled out on the street and smiles, before making it's way towards him for the kill stroke.

It barely has time to turn its head to see what the metallic clang it heard is, before I've tackled it and plowed both of us through a furniture store and out the front of the Chinese restaurant on the other side of the block.

It's not until we both tumble across four lanes of city street, that I've even become fully aware of what I've just done: starting my first fight as a metahuman that I'm not sure I can win. I'm not sure if this "thing" is meta or not, but whatever it is, it's strong. At least that's the thought that goes through my head as it slams both of its fist into my back, buckling my knees and sending me to the ground.

As it lifts its foot to stomp my head further into the pavement, I turn and grab it. With all my might I torque my shoulders and throw. The beast lands almost a block away, but I'm there before it can land to continue pummeling it with my fists.

Is Midnight dead?

That's the only thought going through my head as I continue battering the red beast. Its eyes begin to lose focus as I continue to pummel it. My punches start coming so fast that they are causing small sonic booms, shaking the earth around both of us. Blood is trickling from its mouth.

"Enough!"

Even over the sounds of my now one-way battle, the yell is deafening. I turn to see Midnight standing in the street. Heaving with each breath as he holds his right hand to his ribs.

In the distraction, the beast hurls itself into the sky ten stories to the roof of the nearest building. The ground around my feet slowly starts trembling as I get ready to follow it skyward.

"No!" Midnight yells.

I hear the sound of helicopters and see a spotlight overhead. A voice over a public announcement system says, "stop, right where you are!"

Before I can look back down, I'm coughing on thick grey smoke. One of Midnight's diversions. There's a tiny explosion nearby that I can barely see through the fog, and I feel a hand grab my bicep and pull me downward. It's

Midnight pulling me into a sewer entrance.

I hit the concrete floor with a thud. My eyes struggle to readjust to the darkness. Above, I can hear sirens and screeching tires. Whatever the plan is from here, it's a mystery to me, but I know that we can't stay here.

Midnight shouts to me, "we have to get back-"

Thirteen

"-to my base."

And we're there. I still haven't gotten used to this whole teleportation thing. I guess it's understandable, considering I've gone my entire life up, until this point, without the ability to transport myself any place on Earth instantly with merely a thought.

Midnight lets go of my arm and walks over to a wall unit containing a very advanced looking medical station. He punches a few codes into a wall plate and a series of lasers begin scanning his entire body. They pinpoint the areas of injury and a series of robotic arms begin injecting needles, applying aerosol sprays, sewing stitches and wrapping wounds.

"I'm fine, thanks for asking," I say.

"Give me a break. The only thing you might have hurt tonight is your pride," he says, his back still facing me.

"What is that supposed to mean?"

Just then, I look down and find out what that means. I'm basically naked. While my body doesn't have a scratch on it, thanks to the metabands, my clothes have been utterly ripped to shreds by the carnage that just happened.

"Don't worry," Midnight reassures me, "it's a good thing. It means if any of the news choppers got footage of you tonight, they're going to have to blur the hell out of it if they want to broadcast it on TV. That's good for the whole 'secret identity' thing. Unless that's something you've forgotten about entirely, as seems to have been the case tonight."

A computerized voice declares, "Procedure complete. Three days of bed rest is recommended for all fractures to reset and wounds to heal."

Midnight turns back to me. The machine that administers medical aid has removed pieces of his all black costume around his shoulders and thighs where he had been injured.

It occurs to me that this is the first time I've seen more than a few inches of Midnight's actual flesh. Even the cowl he wears, covers his eyes with white lenses, presumably overlaying all types of computerized information onto his field of vision, but also making sure his eyes aren't ever exposed to anyone,looking to learn his real identity.

"Did you notice something about what just happened?" he asks me.

"Yeah. That machine seems incredible. I've never seen something so-" I'm interrupted.

"This never came off," Midnight says, pointing at his mask, "and it never will. Because this, this, is all I have between me and everything else. If I lose this, if people found out who I am, I'm not the only one is vulnerable. You still don't understand that."

"No, I do," I meekly plead.

"No, you don't. I bet you're pretty proud of yourself tonight. Beating that... *thing*. You think you saved my life. You're on top of the world. Well, what if that thing saw your face? What if it recognized you and as we speak, is at your house murdering the only family you have left?"

I say nothing. There's nothing to say. He's absolutely right. I feel a pit open in my stomach as I realize that that thing did see my face. It might not know who I am, but it knows what I look like.

"We have to get you a mask," Midnight says.

"I have one, I just forgot it tonight," I reply.

"No. Not like that. A real one. One that's not going to rip to shreds the next time you decide to order Chinese takeout from the other side of the block."

I smile. It's the first instance of levity the night's had. I can't really tell through the mask, but I think Midnight gives a smirk too. He has to have. It *was* pretty awesome.

"Do you know what it was about Jones that scared people more than anything?" Midnight asks. "It wasn't how powerful he was, or the randomness of the attacks. Sure, that was part of it, but there were plenty of metas just as powerful who showed up when you least expected them. What truly scared people about Jones was how he looked: like any one else. He wore an impeccably tailored business suit, and no mask. He was handsome and looked more like he belonged in a board meeting, than flying five hundred feet above a city. That's what truly terrified people, that he looked so much like them. People can accept a maniac who dresses in spandex and a cape and flies through the air, but show them someone who looks like a businessman doing the same as he kills without reason, and they just can't process it. That's why you need to look the part. It helps people understand."

"And how do I do that?" I ask.

"With those," Midnight says, gesturing towards the still active metabands on my wrists. "Those things have the ability to create matter. It's limited, but they have the ability to create essentially a suit that covers your face and body. At least, that's how the older metas did it, once they realized regular fabrics get torn up pretty quickly when you're running around at the speed of sound."

"So how do I do it?" I ask.

"Hell if I know. How do you do anything with those things? Scientists have spent the last decade trying to figure out the first inkling of how they work and haven't gotten anywhere. If we knew how they worked, we'd have solved the energy crisis and global hunger by now. All we know is that they attach themselves to a person, and they're the only ones who can ever use them. You've got some kind of bond with them, and you've already figured out a hell of a lot of other things they can do, so you tell me. How do you make them make you a suit?"

As my brain processes the question, the metabands react instinctively. I don't command them to do anything, I simply think about the question that Midnight has asked me. A deep, crimson red covers my hands, then begins it's way up my arms. When it reaches my shoulders, it spreads out in two directions: up towards my head and down my chest and legs. It's over just as quickly as it begun.

"Very nice," Midnight compliments me.

I look over at a computer display against one of the walls in his base, which is displaying an image from an overhead security camera.

My entire body is covered in a deep red, spandex-like material. It's not armor, but whatever it is, it definitely makes me look to be in much better shape than I actually am. The material covers everything except for my mouth, jaw and eyes.

"I'd recommend covering those up," Midnight suggests.

"No. I think it's better this way. It lets people see that I'm a real person. That they shouldn't fear me. Plus, I don't really know how I did that in the first place, so I'm not sure how much control I have here over custom tailored alterations."

"Fair enough. The rest of the suit also makes it look like you've got about fifty pounds of muscle that isn't actually there. I don't think anyone's going to expect that it's you under there," Midnight laughs.

"It's not fifty pounds," I protest. I take another look at the display. He's right, this suit really does make me look ripped. "Maybe thirty..."

"Hrm," Midnight laughs. That's a first. "You're gonna need some kind of symbol."

"A what?" I ask.

"A symbol. Something to identify you. Something unique so when people see you they know who you are," he says.

I concentrate again and a light red circle appears on my chest.

"Wow. So much for originality," Midnight says.

"Hey, it's the best I could think of right now. It's not like you're exactly Picasso with the crescent moon, buddy," I shoot back. Midnight isn't amused, so I quickly try to change the subject.

"Uh, what was that thing back there?" I ask.

"I'm not sure. Whatever it was, it wasn't a metahuman," Midnight says.

"How do you know?"

"Well for starters, it didn't have these things," he says as he taps his finger on the metaband on my right wrist.

"But I can make these things basically turn invisible. Maybe 'it' did the same thing?"

"No. You can't do it while they're active. It doesn't work that way. If the metabands are powered on, then you can see 'em. That's just how it works. Trust me," Midnight says as he sits down.

The chair he sits in is gigantic and swivels in front of an even more gigantic grid of at least a dozen computer monitors. Some of the monitors are displaying news helicopter footage of the battle. Luckily, they didn't get close enough to get a clear shot of my face. Other monitors are displaying indecipherable strings of data that Midnight occasionally glances at.

I'm feeling slightly unnecessary.

"Anything else you need from me tonight?" I ask.

Midnight doesn't turn around. He's entrenched in his work in front of the computer monitors.

"Welp, alright then. I guess I'll be going."

Still nothing.

"Yup. I'm gonna get going now. That's it for me," I say. This finally gets his attention, but he still doesn't turn to look at me.

"Here," he says as he writes down a phone number on a piece of paper and hands it to me without looking.

"What's this?" I ask.

"It's my phone number. In case you need to contact me. No more meeting on roofs," he says.

"Phone number? Are you serious? This is how I contact you? There isn't like a spotlight I shoot into the sky, or a flare, or some high tech gadget that gives me a retinal scan before it alerts you of my exact GPS coordinates?" I ask.

"What? No. That's stupid. Call me. Or text. Doesn't really matter either way to me," he says, already turning back to his work at the computer station.

"This is insane. What if this number fell into the wrong hands!?" I ask.

Midnight sighs and slowly turns his chair back to face me.

"Then I'll get a new number."

"Why did you put that note in my cheeseburger then, if you could have just called me the entire time?"

Midnight swivels his chair around finally.

"To show you that I could," he says.

There's something vaguely threatening about the way he says this. Maybe it isn't that vague.

"Listen kid, this isn't the comic books. Some things are a little bit easier if we don't get too dramatic about them, got it?" he says.

"Got it."

And with that, I use what is likely alien technology strapped to my wrists to teleport myself to my bedroom.

FOURTEEN

When I wake up the next morning, I can hear that Derrick is still home. I look at the clock and it's almost 9:00 AM. Luckily, that means I'm not late for my first day at the lake (yet) which means this new job is already going better than the last, but it does mean that Derrick is probably late for his work.

I stumble into the living room and find Derrick hunched over his laptop, unshaven and still in his underwear. He barely notices that I'm there.

"What are you still doing home? Shouldn't you be on your way to the office?" I ask.

"Huh? Oh. I called out. Working from home again," he says, not bothering to even look up from his laptop.

I stare at him, waiting for him to notice. He doesn't.

"What are you looking at?" I ask. This finally grabs his attention.

"Oh my God. You haven't heard? There was this absolutely insane meta fight last night! The footage is all over the place. The one guy threw another guy right through an entire city block!" he exclaims.

I do my best to hide a smirk. It doesn't matter anyway, Derrick is too engrossed in what's on his screen to notice.

"Wow. Sounds like this guy's pretty incredible."

Okay. Maybe now I'm laying it on a bit too thick and consider pulling back a little bit. Derrick would never, ever suspect me in a million years, but that doesn't mean I should be a cocky idiot about it.

"Yeah, he's all right but not really all that interesting," Derrick says.

Wow. Okay. Never mind then.

"What's really interesting is the thing he was fighting," Derrick says.

"Thing?" I ask. "I thought you said it was two metas

fighting."

"That's the craziest part. This other thing wasn't actually a meta," he says.

"How do they know that?" I ask, doing my best to feign ignorance.

"Because the meta that made him, uploaded a video about it to ViewNow," Derrick says.

"What."

I try to process what Derrick has just told me. The old metas could do a lot of incredible things. Some could fly. Others possessed super speed or super strength. There were even some who could teleport or project pure energy in the way of a projectile. But they couldn't ever "make" something. Not something like the thing I saw last night.

"Here, watch this," Derrick says while swinging the laptop around so I could see it.

He clicks play and the video on screen begins playing. It's a webcam single shot of a person, presumably a meta, wearing a black mask covered by a dark green cross that splits his face into four quadrants. There's nothing discernible about the person himself, and the rest of the room is too dark to actually make anything out. He leans in towards the camera and begins to speak.

"What you've witnessed today is only the beginning. Where there is danger, I will create chaos and no one will be safe. I will finish what Jones started."

The video ends and the screen goes blank. It's the first time I've thought about Jones in a long time. This surprises me, considering everything that has been happening. I suppose it's still just too much to handle thinking about; the man who killed my parents. How he used the same type of devices I have invisibly strapped to my wrists right now to do it.

"I don't understand," I barely manage to squeak out.

"He calls himself The Controller," Derrick begins to explain while pulling up other windows on his laptop screen, "and he's been around for awhile."

"What? What do you mean he's been around for a while? These new metas are the first one's anyone's seen in like ten years," I say.

"He wasn't a meta, but he's been around. Here, look." Derrick says as he shows me an online forum. There's a lot of information on the screen, but from what I can gather, I'm looking at the profile of someone with the screen name 'The Controller' who has posted to this particular forum 14,324 times.

"That's a lot of posts," I say.

"Hell yeah, that's a lot of posts. You don't understand. This guy, this meta, rather, he's an obsessive," Derrick says.

"Aren't you kinda an obsessive about this stuff too though, Derrick?" I ask.

"Not like this guy. There's thousands and thousands of pages of these rants. Everyone in the community knows this guy, because he usually winds up getting himself banned sooner or later because of his insane views."

"Insane views?"

"He's a hardcore Jones supporter. He saw him as a good guy. That 'bringing chaos' to the world 'saved it from self-righteous metahumans who would have eventually enslaved us'. He thinks Jones was saving us from them and ourselves."

"That's absolutely insane."

"What did I just tell you?"

"So this guy has been on this message boards for years defending Jones, the meta who used to just walk up and down city streets killing hundreds indiscriminately. I mean, people with the last name Jones changed it after The Battle just to avoid ever being associated with him," I say.

"Yup. This guy, The Controller, thinks Jones was the good guy all along. And now he's got a nice pair of metabands himself somehow and intends to continue what Jones started," Derrick says.

"Well this is good then, right, all this online stuff? There must be a way to track him down through here right? Login records, IP addresses, something?" I ask.

"Nope. These boards are locked down tighter than most government networks. People on them are paranoid about retaliation from metas whose secrets they expose. Everything is encrypted, and traffic gets routed through a few dozen network connections before it even hits the main message board server. There's no way to find out who this guy is in real life through it," Derrick tells me.

This is not good.

"I'm guessing Electrotown gave you guys all the day off, considering what happened?" Derrick asks.

"Yeah, but I got a new job down at the la-," I begin while taking a look down at my phone to check the time, "shit. I'm late. Gotta go, see you later." Along with being late, I also notice that I've got another missed call from Jim, and about a dozen missed calls from an "Unknown" number that I can only assume is Midnight. Great.

Fifteen

"Where the hell have you been?" Midnight screams into my ear through my cell phone's receiver. I'm driving Derrick's car to the lake to make sure I'm not late. Seems safer than the whole teleportation thing right now.

"I was asleep! Maybe you've heard of it? It's that thing that everyone else in the world has to do once a day or else they start going crazy." I say.

"Well while you've been sleeping, the rest of the world has been learning all about the new friend that we made last night," Midnight says.

"I know. I heard about him this morning from my brother."

"Can you trust him?"

"The guy who made the thing we battled last night? What are you, crazy?"

There's a silence that implies Midnight is barely keeping his composure.

"Not The Controller. Your brother," he says.

"Oh, yeah. Of course. He's obsessed with meta stuff, but he's got no clue about me. I'm sure of it."

"I still don't like it. You shouldn't be engaging in these types of conversations with him. One slip in a conversation and all of a sudden you've turned him into a liability."

"He's fine. I'm being careful. Did you find anything out about this Controller guy that the news hasn't already?" I ask.

"No. But I'm processing through all available data on him as we speak. I'm not even sure he's on the same continent, let alone city, as us. There's a lot of ranting and raving, but not a whole lot of actual information about who he is, other than a lunatic."

"Yeah, I gathered that part. It seems like he's got a grudge now too, which should be extra fun for me."

"That's why you need to be especially careful right now. Listen, I need to leave town for a few days to follow up some of these leads."

"Where are you going?" I ask.

"It's better that you don't know. Honestly, it doesn't even matter, anyway. All you need to know is that if you get yourself into trouble, I'm not going to be close enough to save your ass, so absolutely no powering on your bands while I'm gone. This Controller person is going to be monitoring the police radio, social media, you name it, for any sightings of you. You need to lay low. Got me?" Midnight says.

"Yeah. I got it." That's a lot easier said than done. Ever since I got these bands, trouble seems to find me rather than the other way around.

"Good. Now get to work. You're late."

I pull into the parking lot for the lake with ten whole minutes to spare. Already, today is going about a million times better than the rest of my week. Since summer is still just starting, the lake isn't open yet, which means today is just orientation for staff. Should be nice and easy. How long can it take them to explain to me how to pick up garbage and throw it in a bin?

I lock the car and walk towards the entrance gate when I feel a hand grab my side. Fight or flight kicks in. Hard. This is it. The Controller's found me somehow. I spin around in an instant and already have my arms out ready to summon my metabands.

"Ahhh!" Sarah screams.

Whoops. Turns out it's not a horrific monster or a meta-enhanced super villain. In fact, it's the girl I have an embarrassingly large crush on. And I've just scared the ever-loving crap out of her.

"You scared the ever-loving crap out of me!" she says.

"Oh my God. I'm so sorry," I plead.

"No, it's my fault. I was just trying to kid around. I saw you park, my car's right behind yours," she says.

"Ugh, I'm so embarrassed. I'm sorry again. I'm just on edge a little bit, you know. First day at the new job. Haven't really been sleeping all that much," I try to explain.

"Don't worry about it. I haven't been sleeping much lately either. I was absolutely glued to the news and ViewNow last night, watching all this new metahuman stuff. It's insane isn't it? I mean, we're barely old enough to remember that first wave of metas, but-"

She trails off. There's silence between us for a moment, before I realize that she's just remembered the story of my parents and how they died.

"Oh. Oh. No. It's fine. Don't worry about it. That was a long time ago. I don't really associate metas with... that. I wouldn't be able to function if that were the case. Hell, you should see my brother. He's absolutely obsessed with metas. I don't think he's slept this week," I try to reassure her.

"Whew. Okay. I thought I'd just stuck my entire foot in my mouth. I have a tendency to do that sometimes," she explains.

I already know she has a tendency to stick her foot in her mouth. It's not just sometimes, it's kinda all the time. It's also kinda adorable.

"Have you heard about this new meta that trashed downtown last night?" she asks.

There's a definite smirk on my face. Shit. Eh, whatever.

"Yeah. Yes. Yes. I have," I stutter.

We begin walking together towards the gate to the lake area.

"What's your take?" she asks.

"My take? Oh. Uh. I dunno. Seems like he's a pretty good guy. I saw some of that footage from last night, and it seems like he did a pretty good job taking out whatever that thing was," I say.

"Eh. I think he's over-rated," she nonchalantly replies.

"What do you mean?" I ask, almost choking as I begin. Over-rated? They're super powers! What are they being rated against?

"I dunno. The media's going all gaga over him just because he's got a bunch of powers. There's lots of metas that have multiple powers, what makes him so special?" she asks, and it's not a bad point.

"That's fair, but it's not like he has any control over how the media portrays him," I argue.

"Whatever. I'm sure he's feeling very pleased with himself and smug about all of this," she says. "Anyway, excited about your first day here?"

"Me? Oh yeah. Super excited. Can't wait in fact," I say.

"Awesome. You're going to love it here. I had no idea you were even a lifeguard," she says.

Dammit.

"Oh. I'm not a lifeguard actually. I'm cleanup crew," I say.

There's a few steps of silence.

"Oh. Well, that's fun too, right? You're still outside! Well, I mean not when you're cleaning the toilets and stuff, but still. It's better than digging ditches," she says.

"Yup," I reply.

"I mean, there is some ditch digging, I guess, when you have to help out with the fire pits, but that's like maybe five percent of the job. Tops," she says, not making me feel any better.

We approach the entrance gate together and head inside the facility. The lake itself is private and only accessible to members who pay a yearly fee. In exchange, they receive access to all the amenities on offer, which include separate men and women's locker rooms, showers, a playground for kids, beach chairs, towel service, an exclusive members-only restaurant, etc. It's basically a notch below a country club, and all in all, not a bad place to spend the day. Unless that day is spent picking up garbage and cleaning toilets, naturally. But hey, at least I'm making exactly one dollar above minimum wage!

Sarah sees some old co-worker friends as we head in

through the gates together and excuses herself to say hi to them. That'll probably be the last time I get to talk to her, let alone, any of the lifeguards since they basically see themselves as a separate class from us cleaners.

"What the hell are you doing here?" A voice laughs behind me. I turn around and see that it's Brad Turner. Looks like I was wrong. I will get to talk to another lifeguard here. Awesome. Great.

"Hi Brad. I'm working here. I have a job here," I say.

"As a lifeguard?" He asks incredulously.

"No, as a cleaner," I reply.

"I know as a cleaner, you ass. You thought I really thought you could be a lifeguard?" This question makes him laugh. Laugh and laugh and laugh. I turn to walk towards the group that seems to be gathering for orientation. As I do, Brad grabs my shirt and pulls me in close to his face.

"Look. I know everyone thinks your some kind of hero or something for that little stunt in the woods, but I don't buy it. You didn't do shit and honestly, I think the whole thing stinks," he says.

"What do you mean?" I ask.

"You know what I mean," he says.

"No. I don't, actually," I reply.

"Just know that I've got my eye on you, loser. I don't buy into everyone else's garbage about you." And with that, he releases me from his meaty hands and walks towards the orientation group.

Whatever Brad's view of me is, it certainly does not gel with how the rest of the city sees me. I was 'famous' for being the regular human sidekick that helped save that little girl for exactly three seconds before the credit was given to the meta, and the news cycle moved onto the understandably more interesting story of the return of metahumans. Pointing this out isn't likely to change Brad's opinion of me. He's not exactly known for having an open mind.

I make my way over to the rest of the group of roughly

fifty employees and find a seat on a bench. Everyone seems to know each other and are already deep into conversations. Everyone that is except me, of course. The new kid who got the job through his new crazy, masked vigilante friend hacking into a computer. I sarcastically think to myself how this summer is going to be just fantastic, when I feel a punch in the arm and hear the question, "What the hell are you doing here?" This is starting to get old now.

But I turn around and it's Jim! What a gigantic relief and the first actual nice surprise I've had in weeks now. I completely forgot that he works at the lake every summer.

"Hey man! I'm working here," I tell him.

"Really? That's great. Maybe that means I'll actually get to, you know, see and hang out with my friend once in awhile now," he replies.

"Ugh. Yeah. Sorry about that. I've been-" I get out before he cuts me off.

"Don't worry about it. I know what... happened in the woods was pretty traumatic. I wasn't sure if you blamed me for us getting split up there, or what, so I thought I'd just leave you alone for a bit. Give you some breathing room," he tells me.

I hadn't even thought about the idea that Jim would think I was mad at him. The reality literally couldn't be further from the truth, but I can't exactly explain how my entire life has been turned upside over the past few weeks.

"Oh, dude. Forget about it. I never thought that," I tell him.

"Whew. That is a huge relief. I thought you just never wanted to even see me again."

"Not at all."

"Great! So in that case: where the hell have you been?" he asks.

Whoops.

"Oh, you know. Just busy. Just trying to get everything back in order. I'm sure you heard about what happened at

Electrotown," I say.

Sure, that was only a day ago and doesn't explain why I dropped off the face of the Earth before then, but at the very least, it's bound to change the subject.

"Oh my God. You were there?" he asks.

"Yeah. I thought you knew."

"No! I had no idea. Holy cow, man. You're having a rough couple of weeks."

"Ha. Yeah. A little bit," I try to laugh it off.

"Seriously though. That's really strange," he replies back.

Uh oh. I can practically see gears turning inside his head. Of course it's weird that I've been in two different places, where not only have there been deaths, but deaths caused by metahumans. The first metahumans anyone has seen in a decade. Yeah, I'd say that ranks pretty high up there on the coincidence chart.

"Hey!" A gruff voice yells at us. I've never been so happy to have someone yelling at me in my life. "I know taking out trash and cleaning toilets isn't rocket science gentlemen, but if you want to start getting a paycheck, I need you both to shut the hell up and pay attention for a goddamn minute."

This elicits a chuckle from the rest of the employees, most of whom have less demeaning jobs than Jim and myself this summer. The man yelling at us, I gather, is the general manager of the place, 'Big Jeff'. I remember Jim complaining to me about him last summer. Although he is indeed quite a large man, both in height and rotundness, I hadn't actually noticed his entrance, or the fact that he had started addressing the group. I guess I was too worried about my best friend possibly deducing that I was a metahuman within all of two minutes, when seeing me for the first time in days.

"Sorry," Jim apologizes to Jeff on behalf of both of us.

"Who are you?" Jeff asks, his eyes directed towards me.

"Connor. Connor Connolly," I reply.

"Never seen you before."

"It's my first summer here."

"Well you're off to a bad start. I've got my eye on you," he threatens.

Great. Another person with their eye on me. For years and years, *no one* had their eye on me, and now when I need to be invisible, everyone seems to have their eye on me. Jeff strikes me as more bark than bite, but all the same, his attention is the last thing I need. I'm here to earn some money this summer, get into better physical shape and hopefully fly under the radar as much as possible.

In a world that is teeming with cameras monitoring every corner of the globe, the lake is refreshingly old fashioned in that respect. No need for much security, since there's not much to steal. Sure, kids sneak in at night to go swimming, which is dangerous, but it's a big lake. If they didn't do it on this shore, there are thousands of feet of lakefront they could go to instead, so there's no point to having much security.

The orientation is predictably simple. Most of the other employees have been here summers in the past. Even crap jobs like mine are desirable because, hey, at least you're outside in the summer, right? Once someone secures a job at the lake they don't give it up easily, even after they've gone away to college.

The caste system at the lake is pretty simple too and doesn't take too long to figure out. At the top are the lifeguards. They get paid more than anyone else and basically can get away with absolute murder as long as they sit on a lifeguard stand when they're supposed, which is approximately one eighth of the day.

Below them is the people working the ticket booth at the front. While this is an extremely boring job where you are essentially isolated from the rest of the lake and its employees, it is also by far the absolute easiest job on Earth. Since entering the lakefront requires a membership, they don't even have to handle money. Literally, all they have to do is look at membership cards as members enter and make sure they're the right color for this year. That's it. A monkey could do it if you could teach a monkey about colors. And if it could talk I guess, but that's barely a prerequisite.

Under the booth workers are the concession stand employees. Flipping burgers, frying potatoes and scooping ice cream all day is by no means a cakewalk, but there are some perks. First off, they're the only employees who get to enjoy air conditioning. Secondly, they essentially get all the free food that they want. Not only that, but they control the supply of free food. Nothing makes a teenager more popular in a controlled environment like the lakefront, than the power to give someone a free cheeseburger if they deem him or her worthy.

Below them, and everyone else, is me and the rest of the cleaning crew. We're paid the least, have the worst hours, are outside in the hot sun pretty much all day, have the hardest work, and have to deal with everyone else's garbage. Literally. We not only have to collect, but also dispose of, any and all garbage on the lakefront grounds. When you have a place where hundreds of people are coming through every single day, they're going to produce *a lot* of trash. We deal with that trash.

But honestly, it isn't that bad. For the first few days there, I'm happy to be doing something mindless that, well, helps me keep my mind off of things. The meta sightings haven't slowed down, if anything they've ramped up but, thankfully, they've all been in other cities. I haven't heard from Midnight in awhile, but he's the last person I'll ever have to worry about. It makes sense that he's not around now that Bay View City has stopped being such a hotbed for meta activity. This has also helped me adhere to his whole rule not to use my powers while he's away.

For the first time in what seems like a very long time, I'm just enjoying being sixteen and not having the responsibility of being a meta who doesn't even know fully how to control his own powers hanging over him. Jim and I become close again and start hanging out more frequently, now that I have less to hide. Sarah starts spending more of her breaks hanging out with me too. She even helps me pick up some of the garbage sometimes! If that isn't maybe, kinda, sorta, possibly 'like', than I don't know what is.

She also becomes the first person in a very long time that seems to have the courage to actually ask about my parents. It happens one day, completely out of the blue, as we're walking along the beach. Me picking up ketchup covered napkins out of the sand, and her just asking. There's hesitation, but no pretense.

"So if you don't want to talk about it, I totally understand..,", she starts, and I already know what she's going to ask, "...but since I don't really know, I thought it would be better to ask you than assume: what exactly happened with your parents?"

I tell her about how Mom had arranged to meet Dad that afternoon for lunch. Jones' last attacks had occurred in Skyville so most in Empire City felt a false sense of security. That safety didn't last through the appetizers though. Jones attacked the building they were in. His powers had multiplied. Somehow, he had harnessed a power not seen in any of the metahumans before: the power to release energy directly from his metabands. Later, some suspected he had tampered with the bracelets in some way, allowing them to directly release the raw power they held directly from its source. Some believed that's what actually killed Jones in the end. That this power was simply too strong for him. Or that his lack of super-ego was what allowed him to fully tap into the power of the bracelets in the first place, something which any sane person would never release.

Regardless of how it happened, it was this release that cut a two foot section out of the first floor of the building my parents were in. Ironically, if he had cut faster the engineering experts suspect that the building would have simply dropped the two feet with little damage. Like a magician pulling the tablecloth out from under a table full of place settings. But instead, the slow blast caused the building to topple, right into the building across the street, destroying both. They were the first two of over fifty buildings that would be destroyed that day.

The rest of the story she already knew, since it was a story the entire world knew. The Governor had responded within minutes, but it was too late. So much damage had already been dealt. Some blamed him for much of the damage. While the heat blast from Jones caused a majority of the damage, later studies showed that much of the damage actually came from Jones and The Governor's battle. Two straight hours of repeatedly throwing each other through buildings certainly couldn't have helped.

The Governor tried repeatedly to move the battle away from the city. He would throw Jones seemingly half way around the world, only to have him return to the exact same block, determined on the total destruction of Empire City. The final time The Governor grabbed Jones and took off into space, we thought we might never see either of them again. They were gone for over an hour before the warnings came. Emergency systems around the world wailed, warning everyone within hearing distance to head indoors. Shield their eyes. And under no circumstances look at the sun. To this day, everyone in the western hemisphere remembers where they were during "The Flash". It was unavoidable. The blast of heat was felt around the world.

The Governor had thrown Jones into the sun, destroying his bracelets and killing him. Releasing the power source responsible for the bracelets themselves. The power source that was stronger than anything else the world had ever known, and one which is still not understood to this day.

The Governor returned to Earth two hours later, crashing into a desert in the Middle East. At least they assume it was The Governor. The body was so badly mangled there was no way to ever really even know for sure. His metabands were never found.

I'm so lost in telling the story, that I don't even notice Sarah's eyes have begun welling up with tears. I stop and apologize.

"What are you apologizing to me for?" she says.

"Because I upset you. Sorry. I didn't mean to," I say.

"No, don't ever apologize for that. I'm sorry that that happened to you. I can't even imagine what it's been like," She says, wiping her eyes and regaining her composure.

"Thanks," I say, because I don't know what else to.

She looks at me for a long moment and nothing is said. Usually, I'm incredibly awkward during these types of breaks in conversation, but there's something about her, something about her eyes, that puts me at ease with the quiet. It's something I haven't felt before, but it's nice.

It's a full week before I start to get worried that I haven't heard from Midnight at all. No sightings of him on the news either, although that isn't really that usual, considering his predilection for staying out of the spotlight.

There are a handful of incidents involving The Controller's "creations" across the rest of the country, always in cities where metas have started popping up. While there's a lot of general mayhem when these happen, there's minimal collateral damage, meaning few, if any civilians wind up getting hurt. And the metas always win. There's something suspicious about all of it. It feels like The Controller is just testing the rest of us. Finding out what our strengths and weaknesses are, and making sure that there's an audience. If I've figured this out, I'm sure that Midnight has already done the same.

SIXTEEN

I wake up on Thursday morning and jump out of bed before I realize that I actually have the day off. A day off. I haven't had an actual, honest to God, nothing to do *at all*, day off in what feels like forever, so naturally that means I have no idea what to do with myself and start going crazy.

Derrick is actually at the office for a change so I have the house entirely to myself. Jim's working today so he won't be around. It's been over a week since I've heard from Midnight, and it doesn't seem he'd be interested in spending a day off going to the movie theater with me, anyway.

I get out of bed and take a shower then pour myself a bowl of cereal and park in front of the TV.

TV. It seems like I haven't had time to even watch TV lately. I start flipping through the channels. The cable news networks, that focused exclusively on covering metas during the first meta wave all those years ago, have flipped their formats back for the most part. From what everyone can tell so far, the number of new metas is still relatively low, nowhere near the heights of the first meta rising. I wonder how many more there might be that are just flying under the radar, though. After The Battle a lot of people stopped idolizing all things meta and started becoming very suspicious of humans that possessed powers strong enough to nearly level an entire city.

Along with the possibility that many of the new metas are staying hidden right now, there's also the fact that *bad* metas are already emerging. Last time it wasn't for awhile before anyone that could be considered a 'villain' appeared. There were plenty of opportunists and metas that pledged allegiance to nothing but the almighty dollar. Mercenaries who worked for whatever government, corporation or organized criminals paid the highest amount. While this was looked down upon by the general population, for the most part, it didn't affect their day-to-day lives. A meta taking out a mob boss isn't scary. What's scary is when a certified maniac like Jones appears and has no motivation other than chaos. It's the randomness that scares people. When they can't understand someone's motivations.

The news covers Blue Lightning's latest 'heroics', if you can call them that. Blue Lightning is apparently the name that the meta who showed up at Electrotown has decided to take on. He responded to a domestic abuse situation outside the city where the husband was threatening the wife with a hunting knife. She had barricaded herself inside the bathroom and called 911. Unfortunately for the husband Blue Lighting got there before any of the police had a chance. The wife never even saw him apparently. Later when they were pulling her out of the bathroom she told them that all she heard was her husband, who had been yelling and screaming, banging on the door, suddenly become eerily quiet.

He'd been stabbed over two hundred times. At some point, the coroner stopped counting because it really didn't matter. Only a meta could have done that so quickly. On the news, they had two experts debating the case. Some called Blue Lightning a hero. The husband had put his wife in the hospital before, and it was only a matter of time before he went far enough to kill her himself. The police had been called more than a few times, but each time they responded, the wife refused to press charges, likely out of fear of future retaliation. Some of the talking heads on the TV argued that Blue Lightning simply delivered what the husband had coming to him.

But what gave him the right to make that decision? He posted a defense of his actions on his blog, claiming that the murder happened in self-defense. That the husband turned the knife on him, after he asked him to drop it, and he had no choice but to defend himself. Two hundred plus times, apparently. He chalked it up to his super-speed simply getting the best of him and not realizing just how many wounds he'd inflicted until it was over. For that he apologized, but he also made it clear that he had no intentions of turning himself in.

There was also a small news story about the purple and black, costumed, female meta with the glowing eyes, I'd seen saving people from a burning building last week on Derrick's computer. The one I went to find the night Midnight decided to rearrange my jawline.

Apparently, her name is Iris. The latest news story reported she'd saved another life when she responded to the scene of a very bad drunk driving accident. The drunk was fine, since that always seems to be the case, but the other driver was in critical condition. Iris was the first to respond to the scene, but most importantly, she was able to teleport herself and the injured woman to a hospital instantly.

While teleportation was a somewhat common ability during the last 'Age of Metas' (which I learn from the news is what it's now being called), Iris is the only other new meta, besides myself, that I've seen demonstrate the ability so far. I also take note that she seems focused more on helping others than fighting or even preventing crimes. It's possible she lacks enhanced strength, or that she's physically vulnerable despite her other powers, but for some reason I doubt it. Her actions seem very deliberate. Even if she did lack those other powers, she's putting herself in harm's way regardless, especially considering the uptick in The Controller's attacks.

Stories about these attacks are what takes up probably about fifty minutes of the hour's worth of meta news that I watch. Authorities and other metas were no closer to discovering who he actually was, or even where he was based out of. Some speculated that the closer he was, the larger and more intense the monsters he could create. The only problem with this theory is that the monsters he creates, seem to be getting larger and more dangerous every time they appear, period.

Something else important had also changed: they have

begun to kill. In Springfield, a rhino-like monster appeared during a shoot-out between police and a local gang. A new meta, no one had seen before, appeared but refused to engage the monster in combat. Instead, he tried to talk to the monster. Reason with it. Or at least reason with The Controller through the mental link between the two. This did not go well.

Even after the rhino creature repeatedly smashed and gored the meta, he still refused to fight. That's when the monster turned its sights on the police, gang members and bystanders. In total, the beast killed twenty-two people before the injured meta was finally able to put it down with what seemed like an uncontrollable blast of heat vision.

That injured meta ran off and has not been seen since.

The other incident occurred during a house fire in Los Gatos. As the first responders arrived at the scene, a monster standing twelve feet tall, and made of pure fire, emerged from the now destroyed building. It began throwing balls of fire at any and everything in its path. A very young meta, even younger than me at least, was the first to arrive at the scene. He nobly attempted to fight the fire creature, but the monster was too strong, and the meta was too inexperienced to keep his protective shields up when the fighting became intense.

Icicle, a meta with the ability to control temperature saw the fight on the news and came as quickly as he could. He was able to freeze the air around the monster solid, turning it into nothingness. Unfortunately, he was too late to save the young unnamed meta's life, though. He suffered 3rd degree burns over the most of his body and died at the scene. Even his metabands couldn't heal the damage he sustained. It was the first time since the new metas started appearing, that one was killed. This scared people, and rightfully so. It scared me.

I go to Derrick's computer, sitting on the desk in his home office, with the intention of browsing through his bookmarks to find more information. One of the big meta forums was set as his homepage, so I didn't have to search too hard. After awhile of falling down this rabbit hole, I found the link to The Controller's ViewNow channel.

The videos are all barely decipherable. The rantings of a person who had gone completely mad with power. He'd begun to edit in footage of his creatures' recent attacks to his normal videos to drive home his "points", if you could even call them that. From what I gathered, it seemed to be something about how humans put too much trust in metas. That metas disrupt the natural chaos that enables the world to function. That certain people are meant to die, and a meta choosing to save a life, is no different than a meta indiscriminately deciding to take one. For this reason, he believes he should be the instrument of chaos that keeps the natural order in check.

The words sound familiar. Although there are few on camera appearances where Jones spoke, his manifesto was found and published after his death. Despite the fact that it was mostly the ramblings of an insane person, almost everyone read it to try to make sense of the tragedies he had caused.

It was the day after The Battle that all the other known metabands on Earth stopped working. No one's sure why, other than the obvious deduction that all of them were linked somehow, and the destruction of two pairs caused the others to fail. A seemingly endless stream of scientists tried in vain to get the inactive metabands to work for someone, anyone. Initially it was thought that they responded to The Governor's DNA, and while the government will never acknowledge the experiments it has long been rumored that there were attempts to clone him from samples of his DNA. If they did indeed try, it never worked.

DARPA nearly destroyed half of the Midwest just trying to create a machine capable of opening the bands. X-rays, CAT scans, and who knows what else all, told the same story though: the bracelets were dead. Any attempt to power them on again would prove as successful as reanimating the dead corpse of The Governor.

The last name "Jones" became as almost as toxic as the last name "Hitler". Today, it's virtually impossible to find a person with the last name Jones who hasn't had it changed.

Before The Battle, he was thought to be one of the weaker metahumans. Popping up occasionally to wreak havoc before being taken down by one of the other stronger metas with a moral compass. A year before the attack, he'd escaped from prison for the last time though. He killed seventy two prisoners and guards that day. Those who survived, said he could have escaped hours before he did, but seemed to relish in taking his time to track down and kill every last guard and prisoner who had stood in his way in the past.

The Controller is following Jones' footsteps. His powers might be different, but his objective is the same. Actually, it's even more cowardly, if that's possible. At least Jones showed up in person to cause his particular brand of chaos. The Controller chooses to do it from afar, more likely from his mom's basement, than an evil secret lair.

One thing that becomes clear after a morning of catching up on the meta news, is that I need to be worried. Watching the footage of the meta close to my age, who was killed, shakes me out of my haze and makes me realize just how real all of this is, and just how dangerous it can be.

SEVENTEEN

I call Midnight but there's no answer. Nor is there any voicemail. I'm not surprised.

This morning's media binge has started to make me nervous. Very nervous. My training isn't progressing quickly enough. If the time comes that I need to act to save my life, or the lives of others, from The Controller, I won't be able to do it.

The most striking image from the video of the young meta killed by The Controller's creature was that of him attempting to escape. There was a point where it seemed like he knew he wouldn't be able to win and decided to instead fly away to at least fight another day. He rose about fifteen feet into the air, before he appeared to lose balance and came crashing back to the Earth. From there it was all over pretty quickly.

It was impossible not to watch the video and imagine what I would have done in the same situation. The obvious answer of course would be to just simply teleport out of there; but there's a catch. I've noticed that teleportation, more than any of my other abilities, seems to take the most out of me. I can just feel that I'm drained after a teleportation. What if I were in a battle like this and beaten to the point where teleporting wasn't an option? Where I just couldn't muster the energy to do it?

I couldn't allow that possibility to happen. I needed other options if and when I eventually needed to escape myself. My best bet, despite the failure of the young meta, still seemed to be flight.

With Midnight not around though, my training options were limited. I'd already trashed his bunker just by trying to practice hovering, so practicing inside my house would definitely be a big no-no. I couldn't exactly just go out into the backyard either. That might raise some eyebrows amongst the neighbors.

It wasn't just the attention of the neighbors that I had to worry about. The other problem I had to think about was attracting the attention of The Controller. If I decided to practice in the city, a few quick posts on social media from onlookers would probably be all it would take. The last thing I'd need while trying to practice this relatively new skill, was the threat of being attacked in a major metropolitan area.

No. The only option was to go someplace completely desolate.

The ocean seemed like a good option for a minute, but I imagined quickly becoming exhausted of having to tread water in between practice rounds. Plus, I'd never flown over water before and for all I knew, the rules were different. Maybe it was harder? Who knows yet. That's when it hits me.

I remembered a car trip from when I was very young. Our parents were taking Derrick and I to our first amusement park, and we couldn't have been more thrilled. We were so excited, that we asked how far away we were every thirty seconds or so. While every mile felt like an eternity, I did remember one particularly long stretch of road where there was nothing but cornfields as far as the eye could see. I needed to go to the bathroom, but we were at least thirty miles from any rest stop. Not even a farmhouse. I remember this clearly, because I wound up wetting my pants. Those types of things you don't forget, even after you grow up.

I concentrate and my metabands materialize around my wrists once again. It feels good to have them on after a few days' absence, and I wonder if maybe I'm becoming addicted to that feeling. How could I not though? This slight concern is confirmed when I bring my wrists together and actually activate the metabands. I feel the surge of power, and it is intoxicating after having spent time away from it. Not only am I ready for this practice session, my body feels like it physically needs it.

I close my eyes and concentrate on the image of the cornfields. It has been a long time since I have seen them, but I hope the memory is still vivid enough to allow me to teleport to them. It takes longer than usual but within a few seconds, I feel myself teleport. And when I open my eyes, I'm there. Nothing but cornfields for miles and miles and miles.

This is perfect.

The costume I had 'designed' with Midnight's help isn't activated and I think about just leaving it off. If I was truly alone, there isn't much reason to wear a disguise but in the end, I decide it's best to be cautious. Plus, I should get used to what it feels like to be wearing this thing.

With just a thought, the costume shoots out of both ends of my metabands and envelops my entire body. I don't know why but it makes me feel even more powerful to be wearing this. Maybe it's the anonymity, maybe it's just the fact that with this on, I actually *look* like a superhero. Whatever it is, it feels better to have this costume activated than not, and I make a mental note to never activate the metabands again without immediately engaging the costume, especially since, theoretically, I'll be doing so with the intention of jumping into action immediately and not just futzing around in a cornfield in the middle of nowhere.

I start by practicing the exercises that Midnight walked me through, just raising myself a few feet above the ground and hovering in position as long as I can. The time away from practice seems to have sharpened my skills, or maybe just relaxed me, and I find it easier than ever to comfortably hover and then return to the ground.

I repeat these exercises for about twenty minutes or so. By the end of it, I'm starting to feel really good about myself and more confident in my abilities. I decide it's time to start pushing the envelope a little bit. I can consistently hover at three feet, but what about twenty? Twenty feet is high enough that my natural, human fear of falling should kick in, but certainly low enough to the ground that I should sustain absolutely no injuries while powered up.

I bring myself back up to three feet with almost no effort and rest for a second before starting to concentrate on rising higher. I'm surprised to find that rising up to twenty feet is just as easy now. It requires no additional effort other than concentrating on the idea "higher". That's it.

I slowly bring myself back to the ground.

Hovering feels incredible. The sense of weightlessness is unlike anything I've ever experienced before, but let's be honest: superheroes don't 'hover'. They fly.

I rise up twenty feet again and take another look at my surroundings. There's is nothing as far as the eye can see. I concentrate on my vision and am able to temporarily enhance it to see even further. There's nothing for miles in any direction. I lower myself back down to the ground to think.

Pros and cons.

Cons: If Midnight finds out I'm doing this, he'll be furious. If I can't control myself I might fall back to the ground. Hard. The kind of hard that these metabands might not be able to protect me from. Or I might just keep going into space, with no idea whether or not my abilities would prevent me from dying a quick death up there, just like poor old Elaine DeGrasse.

Pros: Midnight's *probably* never going to find out. Even he doesn't have eyes and ears way out here. If I fall to the ground, I'll survive. I'm sure of it after the experiences I've had so far. If I start to shoot off into space, I can always deactivate them and just reactivate them as I'm falling back to the earth. Sure, that sounds risky and would probably be scary as hell, but I feel confident it won't come to that. I can control this, I'm sure of it.

I take a last breath and concentrate on the idea of flying. Visualizing myself soaring into the air. I start to feel the ground beneath me vibrate. My body feels like a spring slowly being compressed. The ground has now gone from vibration to actual audible rumbling. I have to admit to myself this is the first time I'm scared of my powers, but I need to do this. If I don't do it now, I'll never get the nerve up again.

And with that thought, I turn my eyes towards the sky and launch. I'm temporarily deafened by the air rushing past my ears. My internal organs feel like they've dropped into my feet. Looking down, I see the ground below me, quickly shrinking. I look back up just in time to feel myself break the sound barrier. There's a pop and an explosion of condensation

Breaking through the clouds, the sky above me begins to grow dark and I realize I'm reaching the edge of the atmosphere. Time to put on the brakes. I think the word "stop" to myself. Nothing. I continue traveling higher and higher. Now I'm beginning to panic. There's no way of knowing if I'll be able to survive in space with my abilities. Even if I can, I'm not even sure how to turn myself around. The speed I'm traveling at makes it feel impossible to do anything other than go straight, as if the centripetal force of going this fast is stopping me from even slightly changing course.

I have one option left. The option that I did not want to use. I have no choice though and my window is closing fast. As it is, I might not be able to survive the lack of oxygen up here already.

It's now or possibly never.

I pull my wrists up and smash them into each other, deactivating my metabands.

EIGHTEEN

At first, I feel like I'm floating. Or that I'm a character in a cartoon who has just run off a cliff and hasn't fallen, because they haven't looked down yet. Even now, looking down at the ground, I'm too high up to even perceive that I'm falling.

What I can perceive though is that I cannot breathe. I was right to assume that I was past the point in the atmosphere where oxygen was plentiful, as I gasp for breath. I'm now acutely aware that I am indeed falling. Fast.

With the lack of air pressure up here, I begin to tumble very quickly. I'm in a near vacuum and there's very little atmosphere up here to provide the friction necessary to keep my body from spinning out of control. I try to raise my arms back towards each other to activate my metabands, but the centripetal force from my wild spinning is preventing me from even coming close.

Between the lack of oxygen and the tumbling I feel my vision begin to narrow. The edges become grey as though I'm looking through a tunnel. I'm passing out. Midnight was right.

I'm going to die, and it's because I was too stupid to listen to him.

Nineteen

There's a cool breeze on my face. It feels nice. I turn into it and now it's hard to breathe, like when a strong gust of wind hits you just right and takes your breath away. Slowly, I open my eyes and see the ground below. It's close and getting much closer, quickly. I have maybe thirty seconds before I'm about to slam into it.

I'm falling so fast that it's still hard to move my arms, which are pinned to my sides. With all my strength, I thrust them out to either side and my metabands appear.

Halfway there.

Straining with every ounce of energy I have left, I struggle to bring my arms together, but the wind and gravity have other plans. I feel every part of my body pulling close to the point of complete muscle failure. My lungs feel like they are going to explode right out of my rib cage. With a final guttural, primal scream I push past the wind resistance. Once past that point, the wind pushes both of my forearms hard into my chest without any additional assistance on my part. The now familiar surge of electricity travels through my body as I close my eyes and prepare to hit the ground. I close my eyes, hoping my invulnerability is enough to keep me alive.

Then nothing.

Ten seconds pass and my eyes are still closed. I should have hit the ground by now, but I haven't. Everything is just quiet. I wonder to myself if I'm dead as I slowly open one eye to peek at my fate.

The good news is that I'm not dead. The even better news is that I'm hovering a foot above the ground. I reach out and touch it with my hands. I've never been so happy to pick up dirt in my life.

And with that break in concentration, I fall flat on my face.

TWENTY

It takes a few hours but I actually do start to feel like I'm getting the hang of this whole flying thing. It's unlike any activity I've ever done in my life and requires simultaneous relaxation and concentration, but in the end it really feels like learning to ride a bike. Once you get the hang of it and the confidence that you're not going to fall, you can't imagine a time that you weren't able to do it.

I practice taking off from a standing start and landing with the grace of a ballerina. Then I practice taking off from a running start and landing with one too. I see how fast I can fly along the ground, zooming through the cornfield at what must be at least Mach 1 or Mach 2. After beginning to feel extremely comfortable with my newly honed ability, it's time to tackle height again.

From a standing start, I once again prepare myself for an explosive launch. I'm nervous but I try to tuck that emotion away and remember the confidence I felt while flying earlier. The ground beneath me trembles again, and I take off into the afternoon sky at a hundred feet per second.

I watch again as the ground below me shrinks and keep pushing higher. Faster and faster. I break through the clouds and keep going. Finally after a couple of minutes of climbing, I decide I'm high enough and I stop. Just like that. I have to laugh to myself since it was so easy this time, I feel like an idiot for nearly killing myself before.

It's peaceful up here. Everything is quiet and looking down at this small country town, I feel calm. My concerns seem miles away (technically they are), and for the first time in awhile, I'm just completely still.

Looking down on everything makes me feel powerful. Of course the other times I've used my abilities have made me feel that way too, but there's something God-like about hovering here above everything, where no one can see me but I can see all of them. I can go anywhere from here. Do almost anything. It's an intoxicating feeling.

A feeling that is disturbed by the roar of the jet's engine that, in all of my self-indulgence, I had failed to notice was cruising at the same altitude I am, and now is about to smash right into me. I dart out of the way in the nick of time and just barely miss getting clipped by the left wing.

So stupid. Not only did I almost get myself hurt, I probably would have killed everyone on that plane if it's wing had been torn off by hitting my practically indestructible body. That would have been a nice legacy to have. The idiot who killed two hundred people because he was day dreaming so hard that he didn't even notice a plane smash into him. My feelings of power are quickly replaced by embarrassment.

The plane banks hard to the right, presumably in a late attempt to avoid me. Dammit. Now I really feel bad. I probably gave that pilot and the entire group of people onboard the plane the scare of their lives.

Without thinking, I fly over to catch up with the airplane and approach the pilot's window. He's animatedly talking to his co-pilot and removing his cap to wipe the sweat off his brow. Yup, I definitely scared the hell out of him. I tap on the window to get his attention.

Well, now I've officially scared the hell out of him twice.

Mouthing the words, "I'm sorry", I wave and move back away from the window to give him space. The pilot is screaming now, and it looks like he's talking into his headset. Okay. I think I've done enough damage here, so I start backing away even further and slow down to let the plane pass me. As it does, I see all the passengers crowded around the left side of the plane to get a look at me. Some are snapping photos with their phones. Some look like they have or are about to throw up. I mouth the words "I'm sorry" again to them, wave sheepishly, and fly off in the other direction.

I hover thirty thousand feet above the ground and watch as the jet full of passengers, that I nearly killed, flies off into the distance. I'm feeling pretty stupid and like maybe Midnight was right. I'm not ready. There's a reason why he didn't want me out here just doing whatever I feel like, and it isn't just because I could get hurt; it's because other people could get hurt too.

It's then that I think about that frazzled airline pilot, screaming into his headset. He was calling into air traffic control that he almost hit a meta. Calling in on frequencies that are open and available for anyone with the right radio to hear. Hobbyists. Other pilots. The news media. Literally almost anyone.

There's a loud screech behind me that startles me so badly I actually lose a few feet of altitude. It's in the distance. I can't see it through the clouds, but as I hear the screech again, it's apparent that whatever is making the noise is moving closer. Fast.

Whatever it is, I'm sure The Controller has sent it. I feel even stupider than I did two minutes ago, but now I've got no choice. I look at my gloved hands and they're visibly trembling. I don't know what to do. Teleporting out of here is an option of course, but a cowardly one. If I do, there's no telling whatever this thing might do to that jet full of innocent civilians. So I wait for it to break through the clouds and when it does, I can't believe my eyes.

I still can't believe my eyes even after a dragon barrels into me full speed and sends me hurdling through the sky.

A real deal, honest to God, dragon. Something I never expected to see in real life and here it is, in front of me. Not only that, it's trying to kill me, and by the horrifying looks of it, it should be very capable of doing so. It's probably got at least a hundred foot wingspan and is at least as long in length. And it's mean looking. Really mean looking. Did I mention it can breathe fire? Yeah, it can breathe fire too. I find that out when it start *breathing fire at me.*

I do a barrel roll to avoid the fireball heading towards me. This seems to piss off the dragon as it comes flying at me head-on. I wind up and throw a punch directly into it's gigantic beak. It seems surprised by this move. I'm surprised by this move too. Who punches a dragon? It's knocked back and stunned for a second, but shakes it off and releases an ear shattering screech into the air. It's pissed and I take that as my cue to run. Er, well, fly.

As fast as I can fly, it seems that I cannot outrun this thing. Flying away from it is just a temporary solution to this very permanent problem, but I'm hoping it gives me enough time to come up with an actual plan. I don't understand how something propelled through the air by leathery wings is able to keep up with me as I break the sound barrier for the third or fourth time today, but it does. I guess I also don't understand how a dragon is existing and trying to kill me at this very moment either, so that's fair.

As I tilt up to try to lose it in a nest of clouds, a sharp pain flares suddenly through my right leg. The dragon has caught up and clamped its beak down on my leg. I scream in pain and instinctively start hitting it with my fists. Every blow seems to just strengthen the animal's grip on me though, like a steel vice tightening.

In an act of desperation, I plunge my right fist into its left eye, gouging it. It's a dirty move, but it's an imaginary creature so I think I'll sleep all right tonight. If I survive this, that is.

If I thought it was pissed off before, it's *really* pissed off now. But at least, it has released me from its grip long enough that I can put some distance between it and myself. Distance that it begins to close very quickly. I concentrate harder on increasing my speed to give me more time to come up with a plan, but I still have absolutely no idea what to do. That's when I get hit with a fireball.

The pain is like nothing I've ever felt before. It's a searing agony that I would do anything in the world to make stop.

For a moment, nothing in the world exists except for the pain that I am feeling. If it weren't for the metabands, I surely would have been killed instantly.

In the midst of this excruciating sensation, I realize that I'm falling. Rapidly. I finally feel my metabands begin to kick in and start repairing my now badly burned body. I should be good as new in a few minutes, but only for so long. If I'm attacked again before the healing is complete, I having a feeling I'm done for.

As I tumble towards the ground, I look up and see the dragon hovering into position above me. We lock eyes, well I lock eyes with its one good eye. It lets out a bellowing scream and then dives. It's going in for the kill, to kill me, if I don't come up with something fast.

It's flapping its wings as it dives to increase the speed of its fall, catching up with me quickly. That's when an idea finally hits me, and I realize the way to beat a dragon is to challenge it to a game of chicken.

I steady myself, take one last look at the dragon quickly gaining on me, and then turn my body towards the ground, diving straight down. We're at about twenty thousand feet and dropping, quickly. I can hear the dragon still screeching. It's getting closer. Another fireball comes my way, but I'm able to dodge it this time. Fifteen thousand feet.

The screeching is turning into one long scream. This dragon was born into this world with one mission in life, to kill me. It's starting to get excited at the idea of fulfilling that mission. Ten thousand feet.

I concentrate harder on increasing my speed. This is by far the fastest I've ever gone. Time is slowing down around me. Five thousand feet.

We're over a large clearing, a few miles from the cornfields where I started. The dragon's beak nips the heel of my foot, and I kick it away as I pull my arms into my body to decrease my drag even further. Two thousand feet.

I feel an internal click inside my body, like a progress bar hitting one hundred percent and letting me know that my repairs are complete. I'm back to full capacity. Everything has slowed down to the point where it feels like I'm swimming underwater by the time I plunge through the tree line. The screech of the dragon has turned into a low, rumbling roar. I can see individual rocks on the ground which is now only a few feet away.

If I wanted to, I could now reach out and touch one, I'm so close, and it's at that moment that I teleport. I could have teleported anywhere in the world at that moment but I didn't. Instead, I teleport exactly fifty feet above my current position.

The dragon dives straight into the ground. It looks, sounds, and feels like an explosion has gone off. Trees nearby are uprooted and blown back. I'm still traveling with the same momentum when I fly into the dragon's crater and slam into it with my fists in front of me. I feel myself literally tear a hole through the dragon's body and continue drilling into the ground itself. I'm twenty feet down before I finally stop.

Standing in the crater we've created, I catch my breath as the dragon takes its last; a gurgling, coughing breathe as its eye loses focus. A few seconds later, the monster drifts away from existence entirely, like a nightmare fading away after waking up from a very realistic dream.

This isn't a dream though. What it was, was a very real attempt on my life. One that almost worked too.

I think that's enough practice for today as I imagine home and teleport there, safe in the knowledge that Derrick is at work so I don't have to take the long way home.

And just like that, in less than a heartbeat, I'm home.

And my foot is in the toilet again.

Dammit.

TWENTY-ONE

The next day at the lakefront feels more like a day off than my actual day off, probably due to the lack of murder attempts by mythical creatures. I even volunteer to take the shift cleaning the men's room. No one ever volunteers to clean the men's room. Usually, it's decided by a fiercely debated game of Paper/Rock/Scissors, but not today. Today, the weird new kid seemed so happy just to be alive that he practically whistled on his way to the horrors that await him in the men's room.

One of the advantages of taking such a terrible shift, is that Jeff at least tends to stay off your back for the majority of the day. After he's personally inspected that every urinal mint is replaced and skidmark removed, that is. Lucky for me, my work is to his satisfaction, and I'm allowed to work beach duty for the rest of the day.

Beach duty means meticulously combing the beach for garbage and making sure the beach is clean enough that you could eat off it. I mean, you couldn't really ever eat off it, because of the sand and whatnot, but you know what I mean. In reality, beach duty really means lazily meandering around the beach with a garbage picker and occasionally putting a cigarette butt in the bucket you carry along with you. It's still far from glamorous, but all in all, it's not bad for what is otherwise a pretty terrible job.

The other main perk of this otherwise thankless job for a lot of the guys, is that it affords you a near perfect opportunity to ogle half-naked girls sunbathing on the beach. You'd be amazed at how diligently some of the other guys will work to find cigarette butts that just happened to be within a five-foot radius of an attractive young woman wearing a very small bikini.

"Nice butt," I hear a voice say behind me.

I turn around. It's Sarah. Luckily I'm pretty sunburned

from working outside all day, so she can't tell that my face has immediately become completely flush. She's wearing a bikini, because of course she's wearing a bikini, that's the only way to make me possibly feel more awkward and stumble over every single word I say.

"That's a really gross one. Pink lipstick on it and everything. Yech," she says.

Ohhhh. She's talking about the *cigarette* butt that I'm picking up for minimum wage. Whew. For a second there, I thought I was being hit on by the girl I have a pathetically huge crush on! How horrible that would have been.

"Yeah, it's a good one alright. I think I'll keep it for my private collection," I say.

Okay. That was a little too creepy. Reel it in a little bit, Casanova.

"How's it going?" she asks.

"Pretty good. I was cleaning toilets earlier, so this is kinda like a mini-vacation for me."

"Ha. I have to go up in the chair in a little bit, but thought I'd try to get some sun in the meantime. I see you're ahead of me on that front today," she says, referring to my red face. "Hey, did you see that video of this Omni guy from yesterday?" she asks.

"No, I haven't," I tell her honestly. "Wait, 'Omni'?"

"Oh man. It's insane. Hold on, let me show you."

She pulls out her smartphone and taps the screen a few times.

"Look," Sarah says as she hands me her phone.

It's a shot from a helicopter but very far away. I don't remember a helicopter being anywhere nearby but from the looks of it this one stayed a good safe distance from the fight. Plus, I was somewhat preoccupied at the time with the gigantic dragon to notice something as pedestrian as a helicopter. Presumably it was in the area and came to get a closer look when the airline pilot called in the meta sighting.

At first, you can barely see anything other than two dots

falling through the air, but then the lens changes. Suddenly you can see both of us clear as day. Whoever was operating this camera did a hell of a job following us all the way to the ground, capturing my teleportation and inevitable defeat of the winged beast. I'm unable to contain a smirk watching the footage. It is pretty badass, I have to admit.

"Isn't that badass?" Sarah asks me.

"Yeah, totally. I thought you said he was overrated?" I ask her. I should win an Oscar for this performance. "And since when did they start calling him Omni?"

"You haven't heard the name Omni? What have you been living under a rock or something?"

"Did you not hear before when I mentioned that my life currently consists mostly of maintaining toilets?"

"The news kept referring to him as some type of 'omni-meta', since he seems to be able to harness more powers than usual from his bands. Eventually, it just started getting shortened to Omni," she says.

Omni? What kind of name is that? I don't even get to pick my own superhero name? I don't like this deal. This is what I get for putting a big dumb 'O' on my chest.

"Wow. Okay. Yeah, I just hadn't heard they'd given him a name yet. I guess that's a pretty cool name though. *Omni.* Sounds like a name you'd give to someone that incredible I guess," I say, possibly laying it on a little too thick.

"Plus, now that we've got a better look at him, I gotta say he's pretty hot," she says.

"Yeah, he is pretty hot," I say. Wait. Too far.

There's an awkward silence.

"I mean, if you are into muscle guys. I'm not," I say. I'm not helping my case. "Or guys at all. If you're into guys at all, then yeah I could see how he's hot. I'm not into guys, but if I were, I could see how you would think he's hot. I mean, I know you're into guys, I'm just saying I'm not into guys."

This is getting away from me. Me think thou doth protest too much.

"What I mean to say is that yes, he's an attractive man and I'm secure enough in my own masculinity to admit that, but personally I prefer women. I find you very attractive, for example."

Ugh. What am I doing? I need to just shut up. Shut up, mouth. Sarah blushes.

A scream rings out across the beachfront, "Connolly!"

I spin around instinctively. It's Jeff. I'm so happy to see him and have him save me from this situation, that I could kiss him. Obviously I wouldn't because that would just confuse the matter even further with Sarah.

"Duty calls," I say to her. "Get it? Duty. Doody. Because I clean bathrooms. Okay, I'm gonna go. See you later,"

"Bye," Sarah laughs. It's a friendly laugh. A flirtatious laugh?

"Connolly!" Jeff yells again, even louder this time.

I run over towards him.

"Sorry Jeff, I didn't hear you," I lie.

"What, have you got shit in your ears? Because I'll tell you another place that's full of shit, and that's the third stall in the men's room. It is absolutely clogged to the brim. Whoever was in there really should see a doctor, but that's not my concern. *My* concern is telling you about it so you can go get a plunger and take care of it," he tells me.

Ah, the joys of this job never cease. Jeff turns and walks away from me to go do whatever it is that Jeff does when he's not yelling at me. Yelling at someone else I guess? It doesn't matter. The plungers aren't kept in the bathroom with the other supplies of course, because some kid suctioned one of them onto another kid's face one day, which means I've got to go to the tool shed on the other side of the lake.

I reach the shed and unlock it, using the key from the office. There's a single light bulb hanging from the ceiling to light the tiny shed. I reach for it and pull the string. It clicks, but nothing. Great. Now I've got to try to find a plunger in the pitch darkness of this dank, musty shed. Maybe I can use my phone to at least give me some light, I think and I reach into my pocket to grab it.

As I pull the phone out of my pocket I'm grabbed from behind and thrust headfirst into the wall. Fight or flight kicks in as I instinctively thrust both of my arms out and my metabands appear. Without a second's thought I bring them together as hard as I can to activate them. Just as they are about to meet each other, an arm reaches past my face from behind and a hand blocks the two bands from meeting. A black gloved hand. A hand I know.

I turn around and ever so faintly in the dark can see the two white lights of Midnight's optically enhanced eyes.

"Oh God, it's you. You scared the hell out of me. You can just call you know? Wait, did you clog that toilet just to get me out-" I begin to say before I'm interrupted.

"You were going to activate your powers. You had absolutely no idea who I was and you were going to activate your metabands and give up your identity without a moment's hesitation. What if I were just a mugger? Someone trying to steal your wallet? A co-worker playing a prank? I would have known your identity. Then what?" he asks.

"It was instinct," I say.

"Instinct," he scoffs, "is that what you're calling it now? That instinct could can get you and every one you've ever cared about killed."

"Yeah well it didn't," I reply and move to turn away from him.

"Hey," he yells as he grabs me, "what the hell has gotten into you? Huh? You think you're above the rules now?"

"What rules? Your rules? I never agreed to your rules. You abandoned me in the middle of my training while metas are out there getting killed by this Controller guy, and I'm supposed to just sit here cleaning and waiting for you to come back, hoping that he doesn't come to kill me in the meantime? I need to figure out these powers, and I don't have the luxury of doing it on your timetable all right?"

There's silence.

"You don't know what it's like. Hearing all of these reports on the news. What am I supposed to do? Just wait around until I'm in the middle of it and hope that I can learn how to use my abilities on the fly? Or worse, just ignore a crisis because according to you 'I'm not ready'?"

"If that means preventing you from getting yourself killed, then yes. That's what it means," he tells me.

"Well I don't think I can agree to that," I say.

"Fine. That's the way you want it, you've got it. You're on your own kid. Good luck."

The two white eyes I was speaking with close and there's nothing but darkness.

"Midnight?" I ask to no one. I pull my phone out of my pocket and turn on the light to shine it around the shed.

It's empty.

He's gone.

TWENTY-TWO

I get home later than usual that night thanks to the clogged toilet which meant falling behind on everything else I was scheduled to take care of at the lake that day. There's a note on the kitchen table from Derrick:

"Went out. There's pizza in the fridge. Don't eat all of it."

I take two slices of pizza out of the fridge and put them in the microwave. I'm so hungry that they spend more time in the microwave than on the kitchen table I think. After gorging myself, I peel off my sweat stained t-shirt and head for the shower. It feels good to wash off that day's grime and it gives me a chance to be completely alone and think.

Maybe Midnight is right. I'm anxious to learn all of the new abilities that the metabands grant me, but maybe there is something to be said for taking my time. Every time I'm seen in public as Omni, is another chance for The Controller to learn more about me. If I'm not careful he might learn enough to hit me without warning, and before I'm fully prepared. I'm not sure what he wants, but I have a bad feeling that whatever it is, it is eventually going to come down between the two of us.

I finish my shower and wrap myself in a towel, still deep in thought about the past two days. Midnight is a lot of things but above all, he's smart. And calculating. I might be technically more powerful than he could ever hope to be, but he's got more than a decade on me as far as knowledge about this kind of stuff. If he doesn't think I'm ready then maybe there is actually a reason. He's not exactly the most forthcoming person though.

At the end of the day, he's my strongest ally. Actually he's my only ally. The only person on Earth, or anywhere else for that matter, that knows Connor Connolly and Omni are one and the same. And even though he can be a huge pain in the ass, he's also doing everything he possibly can to help me make sure that he remains the only person on Earth who knows that. He owes nothing to me, yet he took me under his wing without a second thought. Well, first he threatened to torture me I guess but after that, it was all pretty much smooth sailing, until I stopped following his instructions.

I owe him. More than owe him. I need him. I don't know how to do any of this and learning it on my own through trial and error will ultimately take me even more time, not to mention be infinitely more dangerous.

I pull a t-shirt, underwear and shorts out of my closet and put them on. I feel fresh. My mind feels clearer. Without any thought my metabands appear on my wrists almost on their own. I strike them together and become Omni, and teleport to the rooftop where I first met Midnight.

Twenty-Three

There's no sign of Midnight here, but I didn't expect there to be. He can't actually, really be gone. Can he?

I pace the rooftop trying to come to grips with the idea that I actually truly am alone now. I've pushed away the one person who knew my secret and had even the remotest idea of what I'm going through. Stupid.

The night seems so peaceful up here. It's late now and the streets are empty. The freeway in the distance and the hum of the street lights provide the only ambient noise the city has to offer tonight. That and the footsteps of a drunk five stories below me, stumbling home after last call.

"Have you got the time?" A voice asks through the quietness.

"I dun haf ah watch," the drunk replies.

"That's alright, I'll just take your wallet then," the voice says back, with the click of a gun's hammer being pulled back.

Whoa. A real life, actual robbery.

"Screeew you," the drunk slurs back.

"Wrong answer," the robber says.

But before he has a chance to take this conversation any further, I am in between the barrel of the gun and the drunk. The instant nature in which I appear, startles the robber and the gun goes off. The bullet slams into my chest and falls to the ground. I don't take it personally, I'd be scared if a masked vigilante appeared in front of me in the blink of an eye, too. Actually nowadays, I'd take that as being pretty normal, but before all of this, sure, it would have scared me.

What I do take personally though is the fact that this robber had a loaded gun pointed at an innocent man's head. I reach out and grab the gun from his hand and crush it into a ball in front of his face. This makes his lower lip tremble and for the second time today, I'm trying to hide a smirk.

"Call the police," I tell the drunk.

"You call the palace. I dun haf a cell phone," he slurs back.

"Fine," I turn to the robber, "give me your cell phone. I'm calling the police."

"I don't have a cell phone either. Why do you think I was trying to rob this guy?" he says.

"Really guys? Neither of you has a cell phone?"

I'm met with blank stares all around. Technically I have a cell phone on me but it's under this suit, and I don't know how to just take part of it off to reach into my pocket. I don't know if it even works that way to be honest.

"Alright, fine. Have it your way. I'll just take you to the police station myself," I say.

"And tell them what? It's your word against mine tough guy, and I'm not the one wearing pajamas, so I think they'll take mine," the robber says. He seems to have regained some of his earlier confidence, now that he knows I'm not going to kill him, and that I appear to not really know what I'm doing.

"Then I guess we'll just have to bring along a witness then, won't we?" I say.

And with that, I put one arm around the chest of the robber, the other arm around the chest of the drunk, and begin to lift all three of us into the air with the intention of heading to the police station. We're about three feet off the ground when the drunk starts screaming louder than I've ever heard anyone scream in my life, and that includes the mystical dragon that tried to kill me just the other day. I lower all three of us back to the ground.

"What is it?" I ask the drunk.

"Ima scared of heights. No. No. No. Don't do dat," he yells as he squirms to free himself from my arm. This is going to be harder than I thought.

Wait a minute, I can teleport!

And like that, all three of us are in the lobby of the nearby police station, standing in front of a clerk who seems entirely unimpressed that he's just seen three people, one who is wearing an elaborate head to toe costume, appear in front of him.

"Can I help you?" he asks.

"Yes. This man attempted to rob this other man at gunpoint and I prevented it. He needs to be arrested and brought in front of a judge," I proudly state.

"And I'm just supposed to take your word for it based on the word of this guy who's too drunk to stand and no evidence?" he asks.

I can't believe this. What happened to justice?

"Here's your evidence, right here," I say.

And with that I drop the robber's gun, which I earlier crumpled into a ball, on the clerk's desk. He looks at the gun which is now basically unrecognizable, then back at me. Again, there's complete and total silence. The silence is finally broken by the sound of a man vomiting. The man vomiting is the drunk I've brought here, and the place he's vomiting is, of course, all over my legs.

TWENTY-FOUR

After filling out more paperwork than I ever imagined, I teleport back to the center of the city. I need some 'me time' so I hover a few hundred feet above the skyline where hopefully no one will throw up on me. The police wound up taking both of the men I brought to their station into custody. One to sleep it off in the drunk tank, and the other because he apparently had previous warrants out of his arrest. So I was somewhat successful in apprehending a criminal, even if the charges for tonight's robbery might not stick.

"Rough night?" A voice behind me asks.

I cannot overstate how startling it is to have someone sneak up behind you when you are hovering hundreds of feet in the air well after midnight. It's just not something you expect. I yelp like a five year-old girl and spin around to find Iris, hovering right behind me. I try to clear my throat like I didn't just scream like a small child and ask in my best deep superhero voice, as if nothing was wrong: "How did you know?"

"Because there's vomit all over your legs," she says, pointing to the vomit which is indeed still all over my legs.

"Ugh," I say as I try to brush it off, "I thought it would have been left behind when I teleported."

"Never teleport a drunk person without warning them. That whole 'suddenly appearing in a completely different place' has a tendency to makes the spins a hundred times worse," she tells me.

The vomit's not coming off. This is disgusting. I'm not sure what material my suit is technically made out of and how it is that it can resist mach speeds, fire, smashing through concrete, etc, but isn't stain resistant. Wait. I know. I'll use heat vision to just vaporize it!

"Ugggggh! Stop!" Iris yells, holding her nose.

131

Yup. She's right. While vaporizing the vomit has made it disappear, the smell it very, very unpleasant. I try to hold my breath too as the smell is starting to activate my gag reflex.

"And never, ever use your powers to burn vomit. Come on," she says as she waves the fumes away from her face.

"Sorry," I apologize, "I'm kinda new to all of this."

"Yeah, I gathered that," she says.

"I'm Omni," I offer as I reach out my hand to shake. It feels weird to introduce myself like that. 'Omni'. It feels like I'm trying to pass off a cool nickname that I made up for myself, even when that totally wasn't the case.

"Yeah, I heard," she says, staring at my hand but not shaking it. I pull it back.

"And you're Iris right?" I ask.

"Wow, you're not so slow after all, huh?" she says, sarcastically.

Is this flirting? It feels like flirting, but it also just kinda feels like her being mean, too. Why can't I ever tell the difference between those two?

"So, what are you doing up here?" I ask her in a way that sounds a little too much like a cheesy, pick-up line. Maybe this suit is making me a little over confident after all.

"Same thing you are, I assume. Patrolling. Except I don't waste my time with that kind of rookie league stuff that you just did," she says.

"Rookie league?" I ask incredulously. "I saved a man's life tonight!"

"Arguable," she says, turning to look off in the distance.

"Arguable? A bullet bounced off of my chest!" I yell.

"A bullet that might not have been fired if you hadn't scared the hell out of that guy."

"Oh, so now you're taking his side? And by the way, thanks a lot for helping out, since it sounds like you apparently saw the whole thing from up here."

"Look," she begins, "you have to pick and choose your battles. Those charges are never going to stick, and that gun would have never gone off if you weren't there. Kudos for stopping a robbery, but you've got a lot to learn if you think anything you did tonight will actually result in whatever your idea of *justice* is."

Now I'm starting to get pissed off. Fine. I didn't do a perfect job tonight, but who the hell is she to judge me?

"You've got an awful lot of thoughts about how to be a meta for someone who's been one for what, a week or two, at most?" I say.

"I didn't say I have more experience. Just more common sense," she says.

I don't have a reply for that one, but it does make me boil inside. Why does everyone think they know how to do my job better than me? Whether justice is served or not, there's a man who might be dead if it weren't for me, who's safe tonight, and another man behind bars, even if it is only for a night.

"How can you be so cynical already?" I ask.

"I'm not a cynic, I'm just a realist. And more efficient," she says.

And with that, she takes off towards the west side of the city in a blur of black and purple. In all of five minutes, she's managed to completely get under my skin in a way that even Midnight would be envious of. I watch the blur that is Iris continue towards the docks. Maybe she wanted me to follow her?

She probably wanted me to follow her, right?

I should follow her.

I take off after her at supersonic speed and catch up immediately. She might have a quicker wit, but I'm still faster.

"Where are you going?" I ask her as I sidle up alongside her.

"What's it to you?" she asks.

"Maybe I can help?" I suggest.

"Ha!" She laughs before coming to an abrupt stop. I'm about a mile over the Pacific Ocean before I realize I've lost her and double back. I find her crouched down on the roof of a warehouse where I ease myself down next to her.

"What are we doing here?" I ask.

"Shhhhhhhhhh!" She practically yells into my ear. "Shut up! God! I didn't ask for your help, so the least you can do is not completely and totally blow up my spot. Fair?"

"Sorry," I whisper.

We both sit in silence for about thirty seconds before the anticipation gets to me.

"So," I begin, "what are we doing here?"

"*We* aren't doing anything here. *I* am waiting for someone," she snaps back.

Silence.

"Who?" I ask.

Iris rolls her eyes and turns back towards me.

"A bad guy, okay? Is that simple enough for you to grasp and understand?" she whispers at me.

"Okay," I say, "you don't have to be mean about it you know."

Alright, now I can hear myself and realize I sound childish so I shut up. Just then a truck approaches the gate leading to the docks we're watching.

"You're still here?" Iris asks me.

"Yeah I'm still here. I want to help," I tell her.

She sighs.

"So what's the plan?" I ask.

"The plan? The plan is we wait for all of them to get here, then we go down there and beat the hell out of them," she says.

"They're metas?" I ask.

Iris sighs again.

"No. Obviously they're not metas," she says before turning her attention back towards the gate, where there is now a stream of incoming eighteen-wheelers pulling large shipping containers.

"But if they're not metas, and we go down there to 'beat

the hell out of them' as you so eloquently put it, it's not so much going to be a beating as it is a mass execution," I explain.

Iris turns to me quickly. She's fed up and obviously frustrated at what are apparently stupid questions to her.

"Really? Really? Do I have to explain everything to you? Do you not even know how to use these things?" She asks, holding up the metabands on her wrists.

I don't know how to respond, so I stay quiet. This elicits another sigh.

"You turn the dampeners on and bring the power output down a bit. That way, if you punch a regular non-metahuman in the face, you don't wind up knocking his head off his shoulders in the process."

"Dampeners?" I ask.

She's done explaining and instead grabs my right hand and drags my index and middle fingers across the top of my metaband. A series of ten white, rectangular lights glow from the metaband. As my fingers drag across them they turn off one by one until only two remain illuminated.

"Holy crap. I had no idea they could do that!" I exclaim, once again almost giving up our position to the growing ranks of bad guys below us.

"Of course you don't, you're being taught how to use your metabands by a wannabe who's never spent a second of his life actually using them. No wonder you've been dazzling so many people with your *heroics*. You're running around there with these things turned up to eleven. I'm shocked your batteries haven't died on you yet, running them that hard."

"These things have batteries?!" I whisper.

"Battery status," Iris says without averting her eyes from the trucks idling alongside the dock. A series of green, yellow and red lights shine through both metabands on her wrists.

"Wait. So this foreign, alien technology *just* happens to use the same color lights to indicate their battery status as my cell phone? That seems like an awfully big coincidence. I don't buy it," I say.

"I don't care if you buy it or not. These things are tuned to work with whoever is wearing them. They might be more advanced than anything you've ever seen, but they're still going to dumb themselves down to something you'd understand," she says.

"Is that a crack at me?" I say.

Whoops. That time I actually *did* yell loud enough to attract the attention of the bad guys. The bad guys who I'm just noticing now have machine guns. Double whoops. If Iris was annoyed with me before, she's gotta be downright pissed at me now.

"You really are an idiot," she turns to me to say, "now go!"

She leaps off the roof of the three-story building we are perched on and springs into action, quickly dispensing two of the armored thugs closest to us before they, or more importantly, any of the others, notice. Iris waves impatiently for me to follow her. I leap down from our perch and follow her behind one of the trucks, careful to stay out of the lights attached to the corners of the buildings, which are illuminating the previously empty lot, which now has no less than a dozen trucks idling in it.

We peer around the corner of one of the trucks and see two groups of men talking. I focus on them and can hear their conversation clear as a bell, even though they're easily at least a hundred feet away. There's a large ship docked nearby where there also appears to be some activity on deck. Whatever is happening between these two groups, it's quickly obvious that they are smuggling *something* between the ship and these tractor-trailers.

A suitcase is exchanged and one of the men signals for the other men on the ship to begin loading the shipping containers using a crane.

"Dammit," Iris says, "I thought we were going to have a little more time. So much for the stealth plan."

"Wait, what does that mean 'so much for the stealth

plan'?" I begin to ask, but before I can finish my sentence Iris has run full force towards the closest man with a gun. She jumps into him feet first, wrapping her legs around his neck as she twists her body and flips him head over heels. He's barely has time to realize he's hit the ground before a right hook knocks him unconscious.

"Kill them!" Someone yells. It doesn't really matter who, because whoever it is, everyone else seems to be going along with his idea. Bullets start flying everywhere and it's time for me to quit being a sitting duck.

As I sprint into the melee, I notice that I'm not moving as quickly as I had previously. Time is still slowed down around me, but whereas before time appeared to stop completely, now everything just seems to be playing back at half speed. It doesn't matter though, I'm still dispatching these guys before most of them even have a chance to realize what's happening. Without my power turned up all the way, I'm able to punch, kick and headbutt with all my might, knowing that at best, I'll knock out or otherwise incapacitate someone, rather than well, decapitate them.

I'm starting to understand why Midnight does this. It's kinda fun. Actually it's a lot of fun. Within thirty seconds, we've dispatched at least two dozen henchmen (real life actual henchmen!) and secured the dock. I'm not sure if it's the metabands enhancing my adrenaline, but I've never felt so alive in my life as I hunch over, hands on knees, catching my breath. Midnight was right, I am out of shape. Having the dampeners enabled on these metabands is making that very obvious.

"That was incredible," I say to Iris, in between gasps for breath. She turns to me and gives a coy smile. She doesn't want to admit it, but she's impressed. At least a little bit.

"Come on, let's get these containers open and find out what was so valuable in here that these guys were willing to kill us over it," she says as she turns to grab the handle of the nearest storage container.

Even with my powers turned down, I hear the click of the gun and my reaction is instant. One of the thugs has momentarily regained consciousness. I thought we had kicked all of their guns out of reach, but obviously we missed at least one.

The trigger is pulled, and I'm already moving before the sound of the explosion reaches my ears. I can see the bullet and the contrail behind it as it moves from the end of the barrel of the gun directly for the back of Iris' skull. If her metabands are turned down far enough to the point that her punches won't kill a person, then they're turned down to the point where a bullet to the head would probably kill her. It doesn't matter if I'm right or not, because it's a chance I'm not willing to take.

Catching the bullet with my hand isn't as hard as I thought it would be. Even though I'm not able to slow down time as much as I was with these things turned up all the way, I can still get to the bullet before it gets to the back of Iris' head. The hard part is hanging onto it. It wants to pull free of my grip as it flies through the air, and if it can't do that, then it wants to go through it. I can feel bones in my hand snapping long before the sound travels to my ears. Every muscle in my hand is screaming in pain and wants to let go, relax, but I won't let them.

I'm on the ground a few feet from where I started, but the bullet is safely in my bloodied hand. The would-be assassin's gun clicks twice more. Empty. Iris turns in shock and looks down at me with concern.

"I'm fine," I grunt.

Her gaze moves from me to the shooter, and her expression turns from concern to rage. She thrusts out both of her arms and I see the meters on her metabands light up like a Christmas tree. Full power.

"Iris, no," I say.

It's too late though. She's already marching towards the shooter. His right leg is broken (pretty sure that was my doing earlier), and he's trying in vain to crawl away from her. It's no use of course. He's whimpering.

I drop the bullet that's still in my gloved hand and again yell to Iris. My entire arm is killing me, but I thrust it out to my side along with the other one, just as Iris had seconds before. The lights on my metabands begin their climb.

Iris has grabbed the thug by his throat and lifts him into the air. His feet are dangling a foot above the ground as he struggles to try to pull free from the fingers wrapped around his neck.

His eyes are just starting to do that thing where they lose focus and glaze over, when Iris is tackled from behind. By me. The man is knocked loose and falls away from both of us.

"What the hell are you doing?" Iris yells at me as we crash into a nearby warehouse wall.

"What am I doing? What the hell are you doing? You were going to kill that man in cold blood!" I scream back.

"After he tried to kill me!" she yells as she pushes me off of her.

"But he didn't. I stopped him. He's a thug. You're not. You're supposed to be better than him," I plead.

"You've been spending too much time with that Boy Scout. The real world isn't that cut and dry, pal. You think the world is going to mourn the death of some scumbag? Some piece of garbage who's going to do five years of time and then be back on the street murdering for whoever pays the highest dollar?" she asks me.

"That doesn't give you the right to play executioner," I say.

"Do you even know what we were stopping tonight? Do you? Go ahead, you've got your powers turned up all the way now. I'm sure you've got X-ray vision in there, *Omni*. Take a look inside those crates," she orders me.

I turn and look at the crates. I haven't tried to look through anything yet, but considering the list of abilities I've already figured out I possess, the idea of being able to see through steel isn't farfetched. I concentrate on the crates and can see inside them. They're full of people. Lots of people. Not just any people. Women. Not even women; girls.

"What is this?" I ask.

"What do you think it is? It's human trafficking. That's what these people that you think deserve our mercy are doing. Buying and selling slaves," she says to me.

There's nothing for me to say back in response. Maybe she's right. Maybe that man did deserve to die. All I know is that there's no coming back from that decision. There's no way to reverse it if we're wrong. It's not a decision for either of us to make.

The wail of sirens looms in the distance. Someone called the cops. Probably someone who heard the gunshot that almost took Iris' life.

"Dammit," she says, "we need to get out of here."

"Great, running from the cops now, too?" I reply.

"No, avoiding more trouble. What do you think is going to happen if the cops get here and report that there are not one, but two metas on the scene over a police channel? Oh, and a whole bunch of innocent victims still crammed into shipping containers. You think that's an opportunity to wreak absolute havoc that The Controller is going to turn down?" She explains.

Iris is right of course, and without another word, both of us shoot straight up into the air before the police arrive. Once we're above the cloud line we slow to a stop and hover. It's quiet between us for a moment before she speaks.

"Look," she starts, "back there. I'm sorry about that. You're right. I lost my cool. I know I act like I'm some expert on all of this stuff, but the truth is I've been at it just as long as you have. I've never come that close to someone killing me..."

She doesn't seem finished, so I let the moment hang there.

"...and it scared the hell out of me," she says.

"Believe me, I know" I tell her, "The past few weeks alone

I've already had at least two separate incidents where I was absolutely sure I was about to die. It's not fun."

This at least gets a smile from her.

"And another thing" she starts, "thank you. You saved my life and you did it selflessly. I owe you one."

And with that she leans in and kisses me briefly on the lips. Holy hell. Everything feels like it's spinning, and I feel like I'm floating. Well, I mean I am floating. Pretty high up too, but you know what I mean.

"See ya around," Iris says. And with that, she heads east in a blur of black and purple. I just hover there for a moment, bathed in the blue and red lights of the police cars and ambulances lighting the clouds beneath me. Turns out maybe this whole metahuman thing has its perks after all.

TWENTY-FIVE

"What the hell are you smiling about?" Jim asks.

I've just gotten into work the next day and I can't stop thinking about last night. I'm not even used to the idea that I'm now a metahuman, and in one night I get to beat up bad guys, save someone's life *and* get kissed by a girl, no I'm sorry, not just any girl, a freakin' superhero? It's hard to wipe the smirk off of my face, even when clocking in for my job which consists of cleaning toilets and garbage for minimum wage.

"I know that smirk," Jim says. "That's the 'something happened last night with a girl', smirk."

"Nooooo," I say.

Damn. Jim knows me too well. At this rate, he's going to find out I'm Omni by the afternoon.

"Come on, I'm not that stupid. Details! Details!" he goads me.

"Ohhh, details about what?" I hear behind me. It's Sarah, who's just come around the corner of the ticket booth behind me.

"*Something* happened between Connor and a girl last night, but he won't give up any of the details," Jim tells her.

Ugh. No. This is the last thing I want. Wait. Is that a look of disappointment on Sarah's face?

"Oh, really?" she asks.

"No. Nothing happened. Jim's just jumping to conclusions because I happen to be in a good mood for no reason this morning," I say.

"Bull," Jim shoots back.

I turn to him and glare. He knows better than anyone else in the world how hard of a crush I have on Sarah. Regardless of what he thinks did or did not happen last night, it obviously did not happen with Sarah, so he should realize by now to shut his damn mouth.

"Fine. I believe you. Ugh, you're so boring Connor," Jim

says. I'm not sure if he's playing along or genuinely losing interest in this line of questioning, but I don't really care.

"Boring isn't necessarily bad," Sarah interjects.

Is that flirting? Why can't I tell if that is flirting or not?

"Alright boys, I've gotta go up on stand. Have fun," she says as she walks away towards the lakefront.

"We get to throw garbage around all day, how could we not!" Jim says to her back as she walks away. He then pulls me in close.

"Okay, seriously though: what happened?" he asks in a hushed tone.

"I told you, nothing happened. If something happened, happens, is happening, whatever, I promise you that you'll be the first person to know, all right?" I tell him.

"Well hopefully not the *first* person. Hopefully the third after you and the girl. Oh, or maybe fourth if there's two girls..." he says.

"All right, that's enough. Come on, I'm in a good mood and I'd like Jeff not to ruin that for me for one day. Let's go."

And with that, we head into the storage room to grab our garbage pickers.

TWENTY-SIX

It's hot today. Really, really hot. My mood has quickly soured after being stuck in the sun for four hours, combing a crowded beach in search of cigarette butts. Not only does the heat mean near, unbearable work conditions, it also means more people come down to the lake to cool off, which means more garbage. More garbage and hotter sun means stinkier garbage, which means unhappier Connor. Still, I have to admit that it's nice to have a somewhat mindless activity that lets me give some thought to what happened last night.

I don't even know anything about this girl. Is she even a "girl" or is she a "woman"? It's almost impossible to tell with the suits on. She's definitely cute, whichever she is.

"Connolly!" Jeff screams at me.

Yup. I've definitely just been standing here *next* to a garbage can for a good ten minutes or so, instead of *emptying* the garbage, which is my job. My bad.

"Sorry! On it," I yell back to Jeff across the beach as I start tying up the garbage bag inside the can. There's another scream from across the beach. I begin to turn around to tell Jeff that I heard him the first time, when I realize the scream isn't coming from the same place. It's coming from the water.

I can see splashing about a hundred feet from the shore. It's a little girl who's gone out too far. Before I can even process the thought about whether or not I should do something, I see Sarah jumping off of her lifeguard stand and diving into the water. She'll get to this little girl way before I do, considering I can't exactly power up my metabands in the middle of a crowded beach.

"Call it in! I'm going!" Brad yells behind him to Jeff as he runs towards me.

Call it in? The rescue? No! It can't be called in. If it's called in, The Controller might hear it over the police scanner. This is too perfect of a target for him to pass up.

The hottest day of the summer, a beach literally packed with people, and the chaos of a potential drowning victim.

I grab Brad as he comes past me.

"What are you doing? Sarah's got it. There's no need to call it in yet," I say.

Brad pulls his arm free from my grasp.

"Who the hell do you think you are? This is *my* lake and if there's a save, *I'm* involved. And if *I'm* involved, then I spare no expense," he says.

I ignore the fact that the expense of an ambulance actually falls on the taxpayer and/or victim, not him, and try to plead with him again.

"But if you make a big scene out of this, the news crews might show up, and if they do, this Controller guy might get the idea that this is a good place to stage an attack."

"You really think the news might show up? I gotta get in there then," he says with a wink.

That couldn't have possibly backfired on me worse.

And with that, he runs to the beach and dives headfirst into the lake. Sarah has already reached the drowning girl and is calming her down as she carries her back towards the shore. She just got in a little too deep over her head and needed help. That's all. Nothing to see here.

I spoke too soon, because now, there is in fact, something to see here. Something absolutely insane to see here. A twelve foot tall, half-fish, half-man emerging from the lake behind Sarah, Brad and the little girl and heading straight for them.

Looks like I am going to have to get involved after all.

There's absolute mayhem on the beach as everyone with half a brain runs screaming from the water. I turn and run with them, but my destination isn't the gate leading to the parking lot, it's the broom closet. On my way there, my right arm is grabbed. I look up and see Jim's face. He's terrified.

"Where are you going?" he asks me.

For a moment, I almost forget to lie to him.

"Where do you think I'm going? As far away from that thing as possible!" I say.

"But what about the three of them?" he asks, pointing to Sarah, Brad and the little girl who the Merman is quickly getting closer to. I don't know what to say. There's nothing Connor Connolly can do to help them, but there's also no way for me to not look like a complete coward right now.

"I'm going to call the police!"

"Someone's already called them!"

"Who?" I ask.

"I don't know, someone. I'm sure."

"That's what everyone always assumes in a crisis; that someone else called 911. Well, I'm not making that assumption!" I pull my arm back away from his grip and continue running up the beach. I look like the most heroic stickler for the rules the world has ever seen.

I can hear the surge of water the giant Merman is creating from behind me, even as I keep my singular focus on making it to that supply closet and away from the prying eyes of an old woman shuffling past. I turn to look to the sky for just a moment, wondering if Iris, or honestly, any other meta is going to show up to help. Nothing. I'm on my own.

I reach the supply closet and in one fluid movement slam the door behind me, thrust out my wrists to summon my metabands, and bring them together to activate my powers and my identity obscuring costume. To everyone outside, I look like a cowardly garbageman interested in nothing more than saving my own skin, and that's fine. It's not fine for Connor Connolly, but it's more than fine for Omni, if 'he' wants to stay anonymous.

Since it might be a little suspicious if I come right back out of this supply closet in full metahuman garb, I instead choose to teleport myself about a thousand feet above the lake. Just enough distance to get up to speed before slamming fists first into the Merman. And since he's just a creation of The Controller's mind, there's absolutely no need to not be running my metabands at full capacity.

It's almost reached Sarah, Brad and the child when I get to it. They're in waist deep water, and Brad turns to face the beast. I give him credit for having guts, even if it is massively, massively stupid to think he could stand a chance against this thing. He hits it in its belly with his fist, and it just laughs. A horrible, gurgling laugh. The laugh suddenly stops as it raises its fist to deliver what would surely be a deathblow to Brad. Luckily for Brad and unluckily for the Merman, we'll never know, because that is exactly when I strike from above, driving the Merman a hundred feet into the sand and mud below the lake.

The Merman goes limp. It looks completely lifeless. That seemed almost too easy, but I guess I have had a lot more experience since the last time I had to fight one of these things. Plus, a Merman? Come on. That's hardly as terrifying as a dragon. I begin to make my way back towards the surface. There's probably going to be a lot of news cameras, photographers, journalists there now, I assume. Well, I guess that just goes with the territory. Something I, rather *Omni*, is going to have to get used to. I wonder if I can get paid for these appearances?

That's the thought going through my head when I feel a webbed, slimy hand grab my ankle and pull. It's not just pulling me towards it, it's pulling me along with it. Deeper and deeper into the lake. Turns out, this Merman wasn't dead at all. I'm as surprised as you are.

Wherever we're going, we're going there fast. This wouldn't be that big of a problem, save for one thing: as far as I know, I do not have the ability to breathe water. I might, but now would be a terrible time to find that out.

As we travel deeper and deeper into the lake, it's becoming darker around me. I'm not sure if it's just because there's less sunlight penetrating the lake's surface at this depth, or that I'm slowly blacking out. My guess would be a little from column A, a little from column B. Whatever the case, this thing is faster underwater than I am, and I can't fight it, even if I were at full power, which I'm not, considering I'm about to pass out.

There's one chance. Teleporting. I look at my metaband and think "battery status". To my surprise that works. To my horror my battery is incredibly low. Like most electronics, they probably don't like water. It's good to know that some things never change. Actually it's not good to know, when that thing that never changes is about to get you killed.

If I can teleport still, which I'm beginning to doubt, it's not going to be far. I can't waste the little power I have remaining, trying to teleport me and this thing to the North Pole. It has to be closer than that. Teleporting to the parking lot of the lake itself is too risky. Everyone is still evacuating, and the chance of both of us ending up on top of and crushing someone's SUV, is just too great. So I think of the closest place that pops into my mind: the parking lot of the Italian restaurant that's not far from the lakefront's own lot.

The restaurant is a thinly veiled front for low level organized crime, which means they don't actually ever have any customers, which also means it's perfect. I picture it in my mind's eye, and suddenly we're there. Myself and Mr. Merman.

I gasp for air and start coughing, but I'm quick to get back onto my feet. I might have just saved my own skin but this isn't over yet. I still need to neutralize this very real threat, or else it's bound to head right back to where I brought it from. If anything, I've made the situation even more dangerous, since I've teleported this horrific monster right to the point where all the fleeing would-be victims will soon be pouring through.

With both fists up in a fighter's stance, I turn to face my opponent, ready for anything that comes at me. Instead what comes at me, is the last thing I expect.

The Merman is on its back on the hot black pavement which has just recently been tarred. He flops back and forth, gasping like, well, like a fish out of water. He must weigh eight hundred pounds, but he reacts to lying on the hot pavement the same way a goldfish would. Within twenty seconds it's over. He's dead and slowly fades away from reality, like all of The Controller's creatures.

While it's somewhat anticlimactic, I'd be lying if I said I wasn't relieved that I wasn't about to have to fight a mythical creature for the second or third time this week. Taking a quick look around, it's obvious that absolutely no one saw any of this happen. The Italian restaurant only opens for dinner (remember, it's not a *real* restaurant), and we're a couple of hundred yards across the parking lot from the lakefront itself, where all attention is turned towards the lake, not towards the closed Italian restaurant.

Before anyone notices what's happened. I bring my wrists together and power down my metabands. I take another quick look around. Nothing. Nobody. Then without warning, I'm doubling over and throwing up about a gallon of lakewater. Whoops. Guess maybe I should have left my metabands active a little bit longer to deal with that. Wiping the remaining lakewater away from my mouth with the bottom of my t-shirt, I start my walk back to the lakefront.

Once I reach the main gate, it's nearly impossible to make my way through the throngs of police and reporters. Satellite trucks outnumber regular cars in the parking lot. A police officer stops me at the gate. I point to the lakefront logo on my lake water soaked shirt and he lets me through. The place is an absolute circus, and at the center of it is Brad.

An attractive young female reporter from one of the twenty-four hour meta news channels is in front of him with a microphone. A cameraman is a few feet in front of both of them, his lens trained on the pair.

"We're here with Brad Turner, the brave lifeguard who, against all odds, rescued a young girl today from the clutches of one of The Controller's latest monstrosities," the reporter says into the camera.

What? Brad? Brad didn't save anyone! Sarah saved that girl, and if it wasn't for Brad's attempt to upstage her and put everyone's lives at risk, that monster wouldn't have even showed up! I'm not even thinking when my legs start to walk on their own towards the camera. A hand clamps down on my shoulder and stops me. I turn around and see that it's Jim.

"Don't man, it's not worth it," he says.

"What's not worth it?"

"Going over there and making a scene on camera. It's not worth it. We all know that Brad caused that thing to appear by making the situation worse, but you're never going to be able to convince anyone of that. All you're going to do is come across as a maniac on national television, attempting to deride someone who is now thought of as a hero," Jim says.

He's right. There's nothing I can do. There's especially nothing I can do if I'm intent on keeping my identity a secret. It's not worth it. Brad gets the glory for creating the dangerous situation in the first place. Fine. It won't last. The twenty-four hour news cycle will spit him back out when the next big story hits. I turn back to the reporter and Brad to listen to the sham of an interview.

"Now Brad, I know you're being modest here, and obviously you're the hero today, but I wouldn't be doing my job if I didn't bring this up: some people on the scene here say that they believe they briefly saw the metahuman Omni appear..." She begins.

All right. At least *someone* has the common sense to realize that this bonehead didn't fight off a metahuman-created monster all by himself. I feel better already.

"...What do you say to the rumors that maybe *you're* Omni?" She finishes.

What.

"Well I certainly wouldn't be able to tell you if I was would I?" Brad replies back, then winks at the camera.

He literally winked at the camera. I can feel the blood

rushing to my face. Not only has this idiot endangered everyone's lives here today, taken full credit for saving them, but now he's actively encouraging a rumor that he's Omni. That he's me.

I push Jim's hand off my shoulder and storm off in the other direction of the media circus. I need to be alone for a little while. As I push through the crowds of reporters, police and EMTs I can hear them all chattering amongst themselves, speculating as to what actually happened. I should be happy. It was risky for me to activate my metabands here. No doubt, The Controller will be suspicious as to how Omni was able to show up here so quickly to respond. That's not even taking into account the risk of someone having seen me transform.

But I'm not happy. I'm furious. I risked everything and someone else is getting the credit. The credit that I can never have. Midnight, Iris, hell even Derrick unknowingly, have critiques and criticisms for how I'm doing this job that I never asked for. And now when I finally did something right, by myself, some asshole is out there getting all the credit for it.

I push the door of the staff lounge open hard and it hits the back of the wall. It's dark inside and my eyes can't immediately adjust from the bright sunlight outside. I grab the nearest stool and throw it into a row of lockers. I'm not even supposed to be in here as a lowly beach cleaner but I don't care.

"So I'm not the only one who's pissed off."

The voice startles me, since I assumed I was alone. It's Sarah. She's still wet from the lake, sitting on a bench in the darkest corner of the lounge.

"What tipped you off?" I ask.

"I know what you did," she tells me.

My heart stops. She knows. She can't know. Knowing will put her at risk. She must have seen me in the parking lot. I can't believe I am this stupid.

"You do?" I ask.

"Yeah," she replies. "Matt told me. He said you tried to stop Brad from coming in after me and having the rescue called in."

"Oh," I say.

Simultaneously, I feel both relief and a tinge of disappointment. Disappointment that Sarah doesn't know my secret. That feeling is quickly replaced by guilt that I would want her to know, even though that would mean her life would be in danger with that knowledge.

"I just knew that on the news they said this Controller guy sends these things to places where there's already a chaotic situation happening. That he tries to make it worse," I say.

"Yeah, I know. And now Brad's out there, not only getting credit for the little girl that I saved, but also for defeating a monster that he didn't," she says.

"But no one can prove that he didn't, so of course he'll take the credit," I say.

"It wasn't him, I know," Sarah says, "because I saw him. I saw Omni."

Gulp.

"It was just a blur past me in the water, but the speed, the color of the thing. It had to be him. I know it was him. I'm not sure how he knew to be here or what he did to that thing that came after me, but I know it was him. I owe him my life," she says.

Twenty-Seven

They gave all of us a half-day at the lake after a monster hellbent on killing everything in sight showed up, so that was a plus at least. Even if the lake hadn't recently been the scene of a nearly violent metahuman altercation, you would have barely been able to get to the water, thanks to all the media still camped out.

Brad was all over, not only the metahuman news channels, but the regular ones as well, now. It's big news when a human "defeats" a metahuman, even if it's technically not an actual metahuman that he defeated. The world loves the story of an underdog, and there's no bigger underdog nowadays than the human race in the face of the new surge of metas.

When I put the key into the lock of the front door of my house and enter the living room, I'm not surprised to find Derrick glued to the TV and his laptop.

"Another quiet day at the office, huh?" he says.

I give a tired laugh.

"Tell me what happened," he asks.

"You've been online, you probably know more about what happened than I do by this point. I missed most of it."

"So what's your thinking: is this Brad guy Omni?" he asks me.

"Of course he's not Omni!" I yell before I'm able to catch myself. "I mean, I don't know. He could be," I continue, trying to recover from the fact that I might have seemed a little too sure that he's not actually Omni, and if that was the case, how would I know? It invites too many other questions, especially from someone as naturally curious as Derrick.

"I was just kidding. It's obvious this dope isn't a meta human. If he were, the government would have shut him up and gotten him off of appearing on seemingly every TV show that's asked him tonight. Also, even a total moron

155

wouldn't freely give up his identity after what happened to Doppelganger," Derrick says.

Doppelganger. I almost forgot about him. Part of the first wave of metas, his primary ability was the power to shapeshift his appearance to perfectly replicate anyone. Neither hero nor villain, he farmed out his ability to whoever the highest bidder was. Sometimes that was the government, asking him to infiltrate a terrorist cell to gather information, or to sneak behind enemy lines to rescue Americans taken as hostages by foreign enemies. Sometimes though, the highest bidder was a mobster, asking him to spy on their competition.

He made a lot of money for his services, but it apparently was never enough. As happens when you're involved with a bunch of people with dubious morals, he eventually pissed off the wrong person. Since Doppelganger had the ability to look, sound, and act like any person on Earth, he didn't think he had to be especially careful about his identity. Why hide who he really was when he can always change his appearance to be anyone else at his whim?

To this day, no one is sure which group it was that he ultimately crossed; whether it was the mob, our government or that of another country, or any of the dozen terrorist groups he worked for. All anyone knows is that the group he pissed off, systematically killed everyone Doppelganger ever knew or loved. Not just his close family and friends either. They killed relatives he'd never even met before. Old co-workers that he'd lost touch with. His college roommate. Everyone. That's how you get to the man that can hide in plain sight.

"So what did you see?" Derrick asks me.

"Not much really," I lie, "it was too much to take in. One minute there's this gigantic sea monster rising out of the ocean, and the next minute it's gone. Just bubbles rising up from where it was."

"And this Brad guy got the other lifeguard and the girl out

by himself?" he asks.

Uh, obviously I didn't see that part since I was busy being drowned at the time. I quickly think of a lie.

"I'm not sure. I'm embarrassed to admit it, but I just ran once I saw that thing. I was hiding in the bathroom," I say.

A flash of disappointment crosses Derrick's face. He does his best to hide it, but it's there. He thinks his brother is a coward. A couple of weeks ago, I was a hero in his eyes, and now, even though he knows there's really nothing I could have done, he just doesn't see me the same way. But that's all just pride. Ego. I know what I did. I know that I saved them. If Brad takes the credit for it, and if my only living relative thinks I'm a coward because of it, then that is just something I'm going to have to learn to start dealing with. This isn't going to be the first time I'm going to have to put aside my pride if this is my new life.

"Yeah, I can see that. No need to risk your own neck in a situation like that. I'm glad you're safe little bro," Derrick says, and I can tell that he means it. As much as he'd love for me to have returned today with details of my heroics, I know he's just glad that I'm all right.

"Anything new going on there?" I ask, gesturing to Derrick's laptop and referencing the meta message boards that he's got open in multiple tabs.

"Not really. Just people arguing over whether Brad is Omni or not. There was a fight between two metas in Culver. Sounds like it basically ended in a draw but a few bystanders were hurt. Luckily no one was killed," he tells me.

"That's good."

"There's a bunch of jokers on these boards now all claiming that they have metabands now too, so most of the boards have devolved into people arguing over whether they're lying or not, dissecting ViewNow videos from people posting them as 'proof'. It's starting to get exhausting trying to keep up with all this stuff," he says.

"I'm sure. It was probably a lot more interesting

speculating when there weren't actual metas, hurting people," I say.

"There's some pizza in the kitchen if you're hungry," Derrick says.

"Thanks, I'm starving."

I spend the night in my bedroom going through the events of the day over and over again. I keep trying to figure out what The Controller's trying to do. Or trying to prove. It's impossible to dissect the mind of someone who derives pleasure from other people's pain like this though. It's just a game for him. Someone who's so socially isolated that they can't imagine what it's like to experience the pain of losing someone you care about.

The scariest thing to think about is that even if he is caught and brought to Silver Island, what good is it going to do? They can eventually station some metas to guard him, but how do you prevent someone from using their power when their power isn't localized? He can rot in a prison cell for years and still create these monsters any time he wants, anywhere he pleases. How do you stop that? And if he refuses to relinquish his metabands to them willingly, then what? Execute him? What if he can't be killed? Would they just have a bunch of metas brutally beat him to death? Probably. Hell, they're probably even put it on TV at this point.

He can stay hidden away in his mom's basement for years, never having to expose himself. Maybe when we attack these creations of his, it harms him in some way, but there's no way to know. All I do know is that the frequency of these attacks seems to be increasing, and the creatures he's creating are more deadly. Stronger. Faster. I got lucky with finding the Merman's weakness by accident, but I know next time won't be so easy. He won't make the same mistake again.

I look down at my phone and scroll through the phonebook. I land on an entry that is in there just as "M". It's the number Midnight gave me to call him in case of emergencies. This isn't an emergency though, and he was very strict about that. For all I know, this isn't even a number to actually reach him. Knowing him, it's tied to some automated gadget that'll just home in on my location and extract me from it. He still doesn't trust me to fight on my own.

Twenty-Eight

The next morning I wake up to find missed phone calls and voicemails waiting. I'm hopeful for a moment that they're from Midnight, then disappointed to see that they're just from Jim. I look at my watch to make sure I'm not late for work, and then tap the button to listen.

Before I've even heard halfway through the first message I'm already running out the door and jumping into Derrick's car. I have to get to the lakefront, now.

TWENTY-NINE

I get to the lake as quickly as possible. It's before the lakefront itself is scheduled to be open for the day, but most of the employees are there already. Some are sobbing, holding each other. I find Jim in the crowd.

"I got your message. What happened?" I ask.

"They don't really know the specifics yet. There was some kind of attack at his house last night. They don't know who or what it was, but considering the roof was ripped off, they're reasonably sure it involved a meta. His parents were away on vacation, but his sister's... she's dead."

"Oh my God," I say, feeling a weakness in my knees.

"Brad's in pretty bad shape too. He was technically dead at the scene when they found him, but they were able to bring him back using a defibrillator. They think that's the only way he made it through at all. Whatever it was that attacked him, thought he was dead and left," Jim says.

"The neighbors didn't see anything?" I ask.

"It was pretty late at night. A few say they heard a loud noise, but by the time they went to see what it was, the damage was already done. Honestly, I think some of them are lying. Pretending that they didn't see what did this, so it doesn't come back and do the same to them. Part of me can't blame them," Jim says.

"I can't believe this," I say, trailing off. Behind Jim, I see Sarah, sitting far away from the group by herself. She's on a rock and staring into the lake. She looks like a zombie. I excuse myself from Jim and go over to talk to her.

"Hey," I start, "are you okay?"

She doesn't respond. She just keeps staring at the lake.

"Sarah?" I ask.

Still nothing.

"Okay. I can see you want to be left alone. Sorry," I say and turn to leave.

"Do you think this was my fault?" she asks. I turn back.

"What?" I say.

"Do you think this was my fault? That maybe if I had been paying closer attention, I would have seen that little girl having trouble swimming sooner and gotten out there faster? That maybe then Brad wouldn't have come in after me?" she says, her bottom lip starting to quiver.

I take a few steps back towards her.

"No. I don't think that at all. What Brad did he was going to do regardless. Would that make it his fault in your mind?" I ask.

"No, of course not," she shoots back.

"Then how on Earth could it be yours? There's only one person whose fault it is, whatever that thing was that went after him last night," I say.

"Do you think it went after him because he bragged about possibly being Omni?" She asks.

"I don't know, it could have been anything. It could have been that monster from yesterday trying to finish the job," I say, but I know the truth. It was because he insinuated that he was Omni. The Controller's probably smart enough to realize that was just talk, but he decided he had to make sure. And why not? It's not like he cares if he's wrong.

"I just still can't believe it. He might have been an asshole sometimes but he didn't deserve this. And his poor sister especially didn't," Sarah says before becoming quiet again.

I couldn't have put it better myself. Brad didn't deserve this. No one does. And I need to find a way to make sure that no one ever has to again. At least not at the hands of The Controller.

I put my arm around Sarah, mostly because I've run out of things to say. It's not until she turns into my shoulder to cry that I don't feel slightly weird about doing it. I've liked her for so long, but these weren't the circumstances under which I'd always wanted to put my arm around her.

Looking over towards the rest of the employees gathered

near the entrance I see now that they're all huddled closely together now. Something has their attention. Jim's head pokes out from the cluster and looks around to find me. We lock eyes, and there's a quick look of surprise on his face at where I am and who my arm is around, before he waves frantically for me to come over and join the group.

"Hey," I say to Sarah, "it looks like something's going on. I'm gonna go check it out. Wanna come?"

"Sure," she sniffles as we both get up from the rock and start walking towards the group. As we approach there's a lot of commotion and people talking over one another. I ask the first person I see what's going on, a nice guy named John that works the concession booth sometimes and gives me extra fries.

"It's that Controller guy. He just posted a new video on ViewNow," John tells me.

"Start it over!" Yells a voice from the back. There's someone in the middle of the group huddle with their phone out. He drags the video scrubber back to the beginning and starts the video over. Everyone tries shushing each other to hear until someone yells, "Everyone shut up!" at the top of their lungs. That works and the video starts.

It's another video that consists of just a close-up of The Controller's masked face and darkness behind him.

"Poor, poor Brad Turner. He wanted the world to think he was Omni. He wanted to take the prestige of being America's newest, hottest metahuman didn't he? Unfortunately, there was only one way to really, truly find out if Brad was who he said he was. We tried beating it out of him, and he denied it. Said he was just trying to impress everyone. That sounded legitimate, but how can you ever really tell with these metahuman types, ya know? Maybe he was just bluffing so he could get to his metabands and take on my latest creation? That's when it hit me like a ton of bricks: Why I don't I drop a ton of bricks on his sister and see what he's really made of? Turns out, he's made of flesh and bone, just like she was, unfortunately for her," he says, before laughing maniacally at his own horrifically dark joke.

There's a whimper amongst the crowd. We hadn't heard the specifics of how Brad's sister had died. I swallowed hard to fight back the tears that had started welling up in my eyes.

"Believe me, it gave me no relief to kill that poor girl and maim that boy. No more pleasure than a little boy gets from pulling the wings off of a fly. Sure, it's fun, but it's not really fulfilling, ya know? Not like ripping the wings off of the real Omni. That's why I'm asking Omni to come out of hiding and be a man. Why let these innocents keep taking the fall for you? How many people have to die before you're brave enough to actually admit to the world who you really are?"

The screen goes black. The crowd starts murmuring amongst themselves. Many are furious at the video and the nature of The Controller's taunts, but others think he has a point. They ask why Omni doesn't reveal himself. How he let's someone like Brad pretend to be him. Maybe he didn't even have to reveal himself, just at the very least he could have let everyone know he wasn't Brad. That would have been easy enough, they argue. Brad didn't know any better, but Omni is a meta, he should have, they say.

And maybe they're right. Even with Brad hogging the spotlight, part of me was happy that the world thought they had Omni pegged. That would at least mean, they wouldn't keep looking for me maybe. Maybe that would mean Connor Connolly would be safe, and more importantly so would Derrick.

It would have been the easiest thing in the world for me to have just walked back over to the lakefront yesterday with my metabands still active, still in costume, and prove that Brad wasn't Omni. Knowing what I know now, I would have done that in a heartbeat, but at the time it didn't make sense. This is all so confusing to me and it feels like the entire world is spinning.

"Are you okay?" Sarah asks me. I forgot that she was even

next to me.

"Yeah, I'm fine. I just didn't get much sleep last night."

"I don't think any of us did. Tonight's not going to be any better," Sarah says.

"I think I need to go. Are you okay though?" I ask.

"Yeah, I'll be okay. My mom's coming to pick me up," she says.

"Good. Listen. Don't beat yourself up over any of this. It wasn't even remotely your fault. Okay?" I say. She doesn't respond and looks away from me.

"Okay?" I say louder.

Sarah's surprised at my assertiveness. I am too.

"Okay. Yeah," she says.

"If you need anything, *anything*, you know how to reach me," I say as I turn and walk back towards my car.

"Actually, I don't. I mean, I don't have your phone number or email address or anything," she says.

I turn and jog back, "Oh, right, yeah. Here, let me give it to you."

This wasn't how I hoped to finally get Sarah's phone number.

THIRTY

Upon getting home, I find that Derrick basically hasn't moved from where he was yesterday, fixated in front of every media device he could find in the house.

"Day off today?" I ask.

"I called out sick," he says.

Sigh. Of course he did. This is the kinda stuff he's obsessed with.

"How come you're not at work?" he asks before realizing why and answering his own question in his head. "Oh, right. Sorry. Was he a friend of yours?"

"No, he wasn't," I say. There's silence for a moment. Derrick has his back to me, and I can't tell if the silence is intentional, or if he's just engrossed in whatever the latest conspiracy theory is.

"Actually, he was an asshole to me," I say. This gets Derrick's attention, and he swivels his chair around.

"Oh?" he asks, looking at me for the first time since I came into the house.

"Yeah. A huge asshole actually. He's spent my entire time at high school here, trying to make my life hell. He went out of his way to do it. And why? Because I was different? Because I was an easy target? Because mom and dad died and that made me easy pickings?"

"Connor..," Derrick starts.

"And I warned him. I warned him! He went running into the lake when Sarah had that rescue one hundred percent under control. He was the one who told the lifeguard on shore to call it in to the police and EMTs. And why? For what? So he could have his name printed in the local paper that no one reads anyway!" I scream as I kick over the cheap composite board coffee table in our living room. I don't realize it, but I've started crying.

"Whoa. Calm down, Connor. Relax," Derrick says to me,

as he rises out of his chair with his hands out. I've scared him.

"I'm sorry. Sorry," I say as I pick up the coffee table, place it back upright and begin picking up the items that were on it.

"It's alright. You're upset," he says.

"He didn't deserve what happened to him. And his sister especially did not deserve what happened to her. What gets me is that I know no matter what, he's going to blame himself for this. He didn't know what he was doing. He was just being cocky. There's no crime against that. If The Controller wants to try to kill metahumans, that's fine, they can fend for themselves. He knew before he even got to that house that Brad wasn't Omni. He just wanted another excuse to kill. Another excuse to keep everyone afraid. To keep the chaos going."

Derrick comes over to help me pick up the items that flew off the coffee table. We both reach for the same picture frame. It's of the two of us, with mom and dad. There's a moment of quiet recognition between the two of us before I let go and let him place the photograph back on the table. I get up off my knees and sit on the couch, my head resting between my hands.

"So, what are you going to do?" Derrick asks.

"What am I going to do?" I ask back.

"Yeah, what are you going to do?" he says.

"What am I supposed to do? The lake's reopening tomorrow, something about 'not letting the bad guys win' and opening as a show of patriotism. I'll probably go visit Brad in the hospital. I don't know," I say.

"No," Derrick says as he looks me dead in the eyes, "what are *you* going to do?"

He hasn't even said it yet and I know that he knows. The look in his eyes can mean only one thing, and that one thing is that he knows what I am. That he knows that I'm Omni.

"I don't know what you're talking about," I say, but

somehow this comes out more as an admission than a rebuttal.

Derrick's doesn't break eye contact with me. He can see right through me. He always could. I don't know why I ever thought this would have been any different.

"You do know what I'm talking about," he says.

I sit quietly, unaware of what to say. Unaware of how to not only convince him otherwise, but also not further incriminate myself. He starts laughing.

"Do you really think I'm that dumb?" he asks.

I don't respond.

"I'm obsessed with this stuff. I have been even before Mom and Dad died. You know all of that. I know more about metas that probably 99.9% of the people on Earth. Did you really think I wouldn't notice if one was sleeping twenty feet away from me every night?" he says. I'm speechless, but there's an overwhelming need to say something, anything.

"Derrick, I..," I begin before I'm cut off.

"It's fine. I understand. I mean, I don't fully understand, and I'm dying to know a million different things, and I know that families are always the first ones targeted. I know that you were trying to protect me by keeping this from me," he says.

I still don't have a response, but for the first time in the conversation, I feel like one isn't necessary.

"But I am going to ask you again: What are you going to do?"

Thirty-One

It's embarrassing how many tries it takes us, but eventually Derrick and I are both happy with the way the video's turned out. I kept flubbing my lines, or going off prompter and getting lost in what I was trying to say in the first place. Not to mention the fact that Derrick made me power up and back down five times just to watch how it happens.

In the end, we take the least worst of the bad takes and hit the upload button on his computer. The video we've made, or rather that he's 'directed' and I've 'starred' in, is a direct response to The Controller's latest. We tried to keep it short and sweet: If The Controller wanted me, he could have me. Just name the time and place. The only catch: I wanted him there. Not his creations, or monsters or whatever. Just him and me.

It was a public calling out I hoped he would take. All of his power came from the fact that he didn't have to actually ever put himself in danger. He could have been literally any place on Earth when he unleashed the horrors he turned on the world. Derrick agrees with the theory that the size and ferocity of the creatures The Controller creates is somewhat determined by his proximity to them. The further away the creature he created was from his physical location, the smaller and less complex it was bound to be.

The pizza we ordered comes right as we're waiting for the video to finish uploading. I hope this isn't my last meal, especially since I had to compromise with Derrick on the toppings I wanted.

We eat and talk, honestly and openly for the first time in what feels like maybe ever. Now that Derrick knows who I really am, or at least who I can become in a second's notice, I don't see the point in keeping anything else from him. He already knows the most dangerous part. He's glued to every word as we polish off an entire pepperoni and sausage pizza between the two of us and the video finishes uploading.

Within minutes, it begins receiving thousands and thousands of views. Neither of us are surprised, since this was a video of one metahuman calling out another. The professional wrestling equivalent of one of those pre-fight interviews, where they scream into the camera about how they're going to body-slam their opponent so hard, they'll wish they were never born. Derrick was mad at we didn't turn ads on and make a few bucks at least.

I'd drifted off into a food coma from the half a pizza I'd eaten when Derrick shakes me awake.

"We got a response," he says as my eyes struggle to adjust from being asleep and focus on his face.

Actually, we got a lot of responses, the video already had three million views, but what Derrick was referring to was a response from The Controller. The response didn't come via video, just a simple comment:

"Tomorrow. Downtown Culver. Five PM. Between Smith and Warsaw. And don't even think about bringing any of your super buddies or the gloves are off."

I expect Derrick to be giddy. He was finally involved, directly involved, in fact, in a world that had fascinated him for so long. But when I turn to look at him, he's looking at the floor.

"What?" I asked.

"Don't do this," he says.

"What are you talking about? This was your idea."

"I know. But don't do this."

"I have to do this. He's going to be there one way or another, and if I'm not there he's just going to kill as many people as he can to set an example, to prove that I'm a coward."

"I know. I know. You're right," he says, as he finally looks up and into my eyes. "I know what you need to do, it's just that you're all I have left Connor. If I lost you..," he trails off in order to keep himself from choking up.

"Hey," I say to him as he goes back to looking at the floor. "Hey!" Now I have his attention. "I'm not planning on losing this. Someone's gotta bring this lunatic down, and you know as well as I know, as well as the entire world knows, that I'm the best shot at doing that."

This gets a begrudging nod from Derrick. He knows, but that doesn't mean he has to be happy about it.

"In that case, you'd better get to sleep. You've got a big day tomorrow." he tells me.

"You're right. There's just one thing I have to do before that."

And with that. I summon my metabands, activate them and teleport to Midnight's lair one last time.

Thirty-Two

It's dark. I mean, it's always dark here, but this is too dark.

"Lights on," I say out loud.

There is the familiar click of florescent lights as the flickering image of the Midnight's headquarters comes into view.

It's empty. Completely, and totally empty. None of Midnight's suits, computers, hardware, vehicles, etc. Not even a trace that anyone has ever been here before.

He's gone. And he doesn't want me to find him.

THIRTY-THREE

I can hear Derrick back in the kitchen on his laptop when I teleport back into my bedroom. With everything that's going on, I can't begin to explain how relieved I am that, at least, my foot didn't end up in a toilet this time, but I'm still sad.

I stand there with my metabands still active for a few minutes, looking down at myself. My nearly unrecognizable body, covered head to toe in deep red. The meaningless symbol on my chest that has become meaningful to some. I examine my metabands. No matter how many times I look at them, I'm still fascinated with them. Concentrating hard, although not as hard as I had to before, I'm able to bring up the lighted indicators showing that I have nearly full battery power. How the hell these things recharge themselves, I have no idea, but they seem to do it faster when they're off than when they're on, which I guess makes sense. Without the need to keep them powered on any longer, I bring them up together in front of my chest and deactivate them. The Omni uniform retracts into the bands and I'm Connor again.

I stand there for another moment, looking at my more familiar body. It feels so weak in comparison, but there's comfort in its familiarity. This is the thought going through my head when a hand from behind clamps down over my mouth.

Instinctively, I begin to bring my arms together to activate my metabands. I hadn't even had time to make them disappear yet, and while I wouldn't normally activate them in front of someone, whoever this is, obviously knows who I am already. They've seen the bands on me. And they were hiding in my closet after all.

Wait. Who would hide in my closet?

"Don't," Midnight's voice says into my ear. His hand releases from my mouth and I turn to face him.

"What the he...," I begin to yell before he clamps him hand back over my mouth.

"If I wanted you to yell and scream, why would I have covered your mouth Connor?" he says, then releases his hand again.

"Sorry," I say, even though I'm not sure why I'm the one apologizing to the masked vigilante who's been waiting in my closet for who knows how long. I'm positive he does this hiding in the shadows stuff, at least partially, because he likes scaring people.

"Connor?" Derrick yells from the kitchen with slight concern in his voice. Midnight shoots me a look that says the obvious, *don't tell him I'm here.*

"I'm fine. Just stubbed my toe," I yell back towards the kitchen. There's no response back, but I don't hear him get up from his chair so that must have satisfied his curiosity.

"Where were you just coming from?" Midnight asks me.

"From your place. I was looking for you," I say.

"I'm not there," he tells me. Thanks for that Midnight, I kinda figured that part out for myself.

"Where have you been? You have no idea the amount of shit I've been through this past week," I say.

"Actually, I have a very good idea. I was there for most of it," he tells me.

"What?"

He answers my question by pulling something out from behind his back (where and how he keeps all this stuff on him I never understand) and throwing it down in front of me. It's a mask of some kind. A very, very realistic mask. It's of the face of an older woman I saw at the lake during the Merman attack. Wait. It's not modeled after her, it is her. She was him.

"You think this is the only disguise I wear?" Midnight asks, referring to the current all black costume I've seen him wearing every time we've met.

"You were there? Why didn't you do anything?" I ask.

"So you would," he replies. "If I had acted, you wouldn't have had reason to. You were right to be frustrated with me, I was training you too slowly, creating a dangerous situation if you were called into action before you were ready. So instead, I let you out into the world and just stood back and observed."

"But how did you know I was ready? I know I was being a pain in the ass and wanted to move faster, but that didn't mean I was ready. What if things had started to go south, would you have stepped in?" I ask.

"Yeah, probably," he says with a shrug of his shoulders. Unbelievable. I thought I'd nearly got myself killed multiple times, and apparently he was always mere feet away.

"None of that's important right now though," he tells me.

"What is then?" I ask.

"The cage match that you just challenged your online buddy to tomorrow," he says.

"Oh. Right. That." I'd nearly forgotten in all of the excitement of having an actual boogeyman come out of my closet and scare me half to death.

"Do you have a plan?" Midnight asks.

"I do, but I have a feeling it's not up to your standards." I say.

"What is it?"

"Go to downtown Culver tomorrow at five PM and hopefully hit him in the head enough times that he goes to sleep."

Midnight doesn't respond to that. He just gives me his hundred-yard stare. His point's been made: I don't have a plan, and I really need one.

THIRTY-FOUR

I barely slept last night, and I don't know what to do with myself this morning. How do you spend your day when you know that at the end of it, you're going to be facing a person powered by presumably alien technology, with powers and abilities beyond what you can even imagine, and that their sole purpose in life right now is to kill you in the most public way possible? So of course, I don't bother taking the day off of work.

Oddly, I find this to be somewhat relaxing. There's something very Zen about picking up other peoples' trash while contemplating how your own mortality will be up for grabs later in the day. It might seem weird that I went to work when there's so much going on, but Midnight said it was the best thing to do. I'm going to have to get used to balancing my actual life with my life as a guy who can also fly and throw people through walls. At least that's what Midnight tells me. According to him, the number one way metas' secret identities were found out back in the day, was because they slipped up in their own personal lives.

Husbands or wives who thought their spouses were cheating on them, who decided to do some snooping, only to find out that their loved one was actually flying around the city stopping crime. Bosses who fired their employees due to taking too many sick days or showing up to work seemingly hungover because they'd been out all night before getting their head shoved through brick walls.

Midnight was determined that I keep up appearances, especially on big days like today. It's days like this, he said, when someone inevitably starts putting two and two together and thinks, 'You know what's weird? You never see Connor and Omni in the same place at the same time.' They won't be as likely to have those thoughts when attacks happen randomly, but when it's a premeditated fight? People have all day to think about it and wonder who the metahumans battling really are.

There's other reasons besides keeping my identity a secret that Midnight insisted I go to work today. The main reason is my own sanity. Although I can't keep my metabands powered up constantly, it is possible to still lose all sense of who being Connor Connolly is, and start thinking of myself only as meta. Midnight says that this can lead to a whole host of problems, including beginning to feel separated from the rest of humanity. According to him, this is one of the reasons a lot of metas begin killing without discretion. It's hard to feel sorry for a human being when you start believing you're a god.

"Hey!" Jim yells into my ear from behind, startling me.

"Hi. Why are you yelling at me?" I ask.

"Because I've been standing here for five minutes now, waiting for you to notice. In another world today?" he asks.

"Sorry. I didn't get much sleep last night. Just a little tired," I tell him. It's the truth after all, but this I'm going to have to start coming up with some new excuses soon.

"Yeah, I know what you mean. Me neither. You got any plans for the fight today?" he asks.

I hadn't even thought about the rest of the world's reaction to all of this. During the first wave of metas, there were occasionally premeditated battles, but it was very rare. Almost all of them seemed to happen at random. People were lucky if the news crews got there in time to get a glimpse of little more than the aftermath. It's different now. Back then, how would you have contacted another meta even if you did want to fight him or her? Now all you have to do is send a message through social media. Even though I've basically grown up with social media as my reality, it was still weird to think of metas being able to use it for things like setting up a fight that might destroy a city block or three.

Downtown Culver had already been evacuated late last night. After 'The Battle', people take metahuman evacuation warnings very seriously. After the evacuations, the media was able to get into the area and install ballistic-proof cameras on the street, rooftops, etc. The government allows this, and actually encourages it, since in theory, it keeps those with more curiosity than sense far away if they can just watch on TV.

That's not enough though, of course. In addition to the robotically controlled cameras, there's also camera-equipped drones that are already circling the area. Some are the military's, used for information reconnaissance in case they ever find themselves pitted against one of us some day, but most are run by the media corporations, making sure they're able to get a good vantage point of the fight even if it strays outside of the predetermined area.

In the old days, helicopters used to do this job. I can't even begin to tell you how many helicopters and their crews, were lost during those times. They'd get too close, or a meta would decide to use one of them as a weapon itself and that was that. By the end of the first wave of metas, there was no one left crazy enough to go near a fight with a helicopter even if you offered them a million dollars. And companies did.

I feign ignorance to Jim.

"Oh, that's today? I thought it was tomorrow," I say.

"What? No it's not tomorrow, you idiot. It's today. Five o'clock," he says.

I might have gone too far with pretending not to be aware. Everyone is aware. Businesses are closing early all over the country, just because they know everyone will be glued to the nearest screen to watch. The lakefront is one such business, so of course I would know that the fight would be today.

"Right. Stupid. Like I said, I didn't get much sleep last night," I say.

"I'm having people over my place to watch it if you wanna come by. We're getting pizza," he says.

"Ah, thanks man but I'm pretty beat. I think I'm just gonna watch it from my couch with Derrick," I lie.

"Suit yourself. Sarah's coming," he tells me.

"She is?" I ask, probably too quickly.

"Yup. Does that change your mind?" he says with a smirk.

Is there a way to be two places at once? No. Stop it. Focus. You've got a meta to defeat today, this isn't the time to try to concoct a way just to be in the same room, at the same time, as Sarah.

"Nah, I can't. I already promised Derrick," I say, somewhat crestfallen, even though I have no choice.

"Fair enough. Well I'm getting out of here a little bit early to go home and set up," Jim says.

"What time is it?" I ask as I look at my phone's clock.

Shit! It's already four! How did this happen? Right, because I spent a few hours today staring at the sand and the water, wondering if it'd be the last time I'd ever see them again. So stupid. I'm late.

"I didn't realize how late it is. I've got to get out of here too," I say.

"Relax, these things always start late. You remember how it is," Jim says, "See you tomorrow?"

"I hope so," I say by accident. Luckily, Jim doesn't notice that that's a weird thing to say. Probably because I'm being paranoid, and he isn't thinking that the guy with two garbage bags in his hands is on his way to go possibly save the world. Or at least a city. Well, at least the downtown area of a city. But it is a very nice city.

THIRTY-FIVE

I teleport into Downtown Culver and meet Midnight with about ten minutes to spare. This isn't because I'm trying to be particularly punctual. If anything, getting here early is a liability, as the earlier we're here, the sooner the drones will spot us. This gives The Controller the edge early on in this little game if he plans to play dirty, which I can assume, he does.

Luckily for me, I've actually made a little detour. Midnight's asked me to meet him a few blocks from the actual place I'm set to confront The Controller face to face for the first time. We're in a small, extremely dingy apartment that looks like it hasn't been cleaned or inhabited by anything that walks upright in a very long time. I have no idea why we're here, but I don't question it. His reasons for this are his own and at this point, I don't even ask. If he's not willing to tell me on his own, there's no point.

"You're probably wondering why I asked you to bring us here first," Midnight says.

"Yeah actually, I was." Can he read minds now?

"We're here because of this," he says, opening up a closet to reveal an extremely elaborate, but also very foreign looking device. Half of it looks like a computer or server rack, and the other half looks like an amalgamation of random household appliances, like microwaves and mini refrigerators.

"Ok," I say, "of course. That makes sense."

Midnight turns away from meddling with the device to give me a look that lets me know, he knows I don't know what I'm talking about.

"Alright, I'll bite. What is this?" I ask.

"It's an EMP bomb. Do you know what that is?" he says.

"Electromagnetic pulse. Of course. We learned about them in school. They make everything electronic that's nearby go haywire and shutdown when they go off. They tried to use them to stop the metas way back, but it never worked. Oh my God, did you actually make one that can shut down metabands?" I ask.

"No, but it can shut down the next best thing," he says as he pulls a lever and the device whirs into action. The lights dim, and then go out completely.

"Great," I say, "so at least we're in the dark now. That's your plan?"

And with the end of that sentence, there is an absolutely enormous crash outside the nearest window. I probably shouldn't, but I run to it immediately to see what I just heard. It's a news station drone. Looks like it crashed nose first directly into the pavement.

"There you go," Midnight says.

"Disabling drones? I'm guessing all the stationary cameras too?" I ask.

"Yes," he says.

"Brilliant idea," I say back. Midnight can tell I'm not actually sure why he did this.

"Look, if we're going to pull off the plan that we discussed, we're going to need the rest of the world to not be privy to it. At least not yet. Not until it's done and they fully understood. Otherwise, The Controller is going to be the least of our problems," he tells me.

"Okay," I say, "I trust you."

"Good," Midnight says, as he gives me a slap on the shoulder that is maybe just a little bit too hard, even with my metabands turned up full strength. And with that, a grappling hook flies past my head and out through the window from seemingly nowhere, with Midnight following quickly behind it.

I'm on my own now.

THIRTY-SIX

I was expecting that the streets would be quiet. That tends to happen when the government issues a mandatory, city-wide evacuation, but that doesn't mean it's still not creepy as hell. A pigeon flies out of a nearby garbage can as I walk down First Avenue, and I nearly die of a heart attack before the battle even starts. It's five o'clock and there's no sign of The Controller. I consider using my enhanced vision ability to begin looking through the walls of the various buildings, but I'm so paranoid about wasting any of my energy that I hold off. I still haven't fully tested these things, and I have no idea what their power limits actually are yet.

In the distance, I think I can hear something. A scrapping sound. With the quiet right now, I can't tell if it's my mind playing tricks on me, a sound being made by some automated machine left on, or a warning I should start taking very seriously. I have my answer a few seconds later as a fifty foot long snake, that's at least four feet in diameter, comes slithering quickly around the corner of Fifth Street. The coloring is unnatural and unnerving. All florescent pinks and greens. One of the few things that I know about snakes is that brightly colored ones were usually the most dangerous. This one is brighter than anything I've ever seen existing in nature. Oh, and it's also about the size of a tanker truck.

The snake stops half a block away from where I am standing and begins to rear its head up. It opens its mouth with a hiss, baring its fangs. I'm frozen it place, staring. I've always hated snakes. Before I can even process that thought, it strikes. I dodge to the right and it misses me, but just barely. The speed of it is unbelievable, even to me.

The hell with conserving power I think as I leap off of the curb and into the sky, hoping to gain an advantage over this thing from the air. Presuming it can't fly of course.

Luckily, I find out very quickly that it can't fly. Unluckily, I find out that what it can do is climb up the side of buildings like an insect. I have no idea how it's doing this, but these are stupid questions to ponder when you're looking at something that shouldn't exist in the first place, and it's trying to kill you.

Hovering about five stories in the air, I move away from the building it is quickly climbing up and move around the corner of the block. I need to give myself some breathing room, so I can consider what my next move is going to be. My first few haven't been very impressive.

"Just keep it busy," Midnight's voice crackles over my earpiece. I'd forgot I was even wearing this and the sound of his voice startles me.

"Yeah, I kinda don't have much of a choice so don't worry about that. How are things going on your end?" I ask.

"I've found The Controller. He's in an apartment on Third Avenue and Fifth Street," he says.

The snake rounds the corner of the building and locks its eyes on me. It hisses again, showing me it's fangs that must be half the size of my entire body. I turn and fly down the street as quickly as I can. Glancing back, I can see it moving along the sides of the buildings. Not only is it keeping up, it seems to be gaining on me.

"I don't know how much longer I can play cat and mouse with this thing. Whatever your plan is to take this guy down, you need to do it, now!" I yell. It's the first time I've barked orders at Midnight, but the stakes have never been this high before.

The snake is now right alongside me. I turn to change direction, but before I can react, it's in the air. It might not be able to fly but it can jump. Pretty far too. I duck just in time to miss its razor sharp fangs and begin a controlled fall back towards the ground. The snake's instincts are quick though, and it twists and contorts its body to compensate for its near miss.

Its tail hits my back hard and unexpectedly. As we both continue falling, I feel the very end of its tail wrap around my leg. Quickly, the rest of its body follows suit. By the time we both hit the ground my legs are already wrapped up. Now that I'm partially immobilized, its head makes another attempt at removing mine. I see the mouth coming at me, and I'm able to dodge it and strike it in the side of its face with my fist. The tension from the snake's tail wrapped around my legs loosens for a second, and I think I have my chance to escape but before I can react it, comes back, tighter than before.

The snake pulls its head back up and hisses at me. I can tell that its not happy. It goes to make another strike, and I think it misses, but it hasn't missed at all. Instead, it's circling around my body, faster and faster, wrapping me up in its grip. I begin hammering away at it with my fists but to no avail. Every time I feel its grip loosen in the slightest, it comes back even harder an instant later. Within a few seconds, it has my entire body wrapped up.

The Controller might be too cowardly to face me in person, but he's close enough that his creations are stronger than ever. Despite my struggling, I cannot free myself even an inch from the snake's vice-like hold. As it finishes wrapping around my head, everything goes dark. That's when I feel it start to squeeze. I can't breathe and with every exhale, the grip just becomes tighter, taking up the space vacated by the air that was previously in my lungs.

Everything starts to feel cold. My body is beginning to go numb. I might have a lot of abilities, but I still need to breathe oxygen. All I can think about is how cold this feels. My mind focuses on this singular thought, and I begin to feel even colder, like I'm surrounded by ice. The snake is still wrapped around me tightly, but I can feel it beginning to squirm. Its grip loosens slightly, allowing for light, and more importantly, air to seep in, and I realize that I *am* surrounded by ice. Lots of it. The snake's entire body is slowly freezing, starting with the areas where it is making contact with me.

I'm doing this. I have the power to freeze things. Who

knew? Maybe I'm wrong about the whole 'needing oxygen' thing too, and I just don't know it yet.

While the snake's grip has loosened, this isn't over. I concentrate harder on the cold, imagining the entire snake turning to one big ice sculpture. It lets out an horrific squealing sound as the freezing continues its path towards the snakes head. The sound of crackling ice all around me echoes inside the trap it has created with its own body. The squeal stops, as does the sound of icicles forming. Then, with as much strength as I can muster, I throw both fists deep into the ice.

The snake shatters into thousands of pieces. They rain down upon me as I fall to my knees, gasping for breath. I can feel the color slowly returning to the part of my face which isn't obscured by a cowl.

It's quiet again and all I can hear are my own strained gasps for air, but then another sound breaks the silence. The sound of two hands, slowly clapping. I look up and there he is.

The Controller.

"Very, very well done," he says. I'm still too out of breath to even respond. "It was a close one, but that was one of my strongest creations yet, so my hat is off to you, good sir," he says, offering a patronizing bow.

I begin to finally catch my breath and work my way up to my feet, slowly steadying myself as I rise. What's going on? How is he here? Midnight had him cornered in an apartment. This doesn't make any sense, but I can't let on that there is a plan.

"You're actually here. I thought you were too much of a coward to fight your own battles. That you'd rather have your little video game creatures do it for you," I say.

"Those are mighty strong words for someone who'd let an old man do his fighting for him," The Controller says.

"What are you talking about?" I say, trying my best to bluff.

"You know what I'm talking about. Your pal Midnight. The one who's prowling around my apartment right now. Well, it's not actually my apartment any more. I think I'm going to let the lease expire," he says.

And with that I hear the muffled boom of a very large explosion a few blocks away. I look in The Controller's eyes, and I know he's not bluffing.

"You know, I've gotten very good at making these creations of mine. So good in fact, that I was able to make an absolute *perfect* replica of even myself. I had him standing at that window with binoculars, watching this whole fight. It was very convincing, if I do say so myself. I'm sure your friend Midnight would agree, if he were still around to do so."

Midnight. I'm temporarily dizzy with the mix of emotions that rush into my head, before they're overcome by the most primal one: rage. I rush at The Controller and begin pummeling him. My fists are flying so fast that they become a blur, even to me. And yet the whole time he just laughs. Even through the gurgle of blood filling his mouth, he laughs. And then he disappears.

Stupid. I should have known this would be another illusion. Another "creation" of his.

"Face me you bastard!" I scream. The scream bounces off the surrounding buildings and travels for blocks.

"Fine!" A yell comes from behind me. I turn to face it and it's The Controller a block away. Or at least it appears to be The Controller. In all likelihood, it's another copy, so I avoid the risk of expending even more energy fighting a shadow.

"This is the real me. You don't believe me though, do you?" he says. "That's fair. I wouldn't believe me either. But here's the thing; if me and you are going to have a fight, a real, no holds barred, knock'em down, drag'em out fight, then I need to know that it's going to be a fair one."

"A fair one? You use deception and murder rather than having the courage to even be in the same county while you're doing it. You're a coward," I yell down the street.

"A coward? Says the man hiding behind a mask and using technology from beyond this world? I'm not the coward. I'm not any different from you. You use your abilities, and I use mine. So if it's a fair fight you want, with me, the real me, you've got it. But unless you're going to take those bands off and stop using your powers, I don't know why you expect me to behave any differently," he says.

I've heard enough. Whether this is the real Controller or not, I'm going to bash his skull in. At least I'll feel better. I begin charging towards him. He doesn't move. Lying to me again, no doubt. This isn't the real him.

I'm halfway there, when he begins rising from the street and into the air. I begin to leap into the air myself after him when I stop. He's not flying away, he's flying into position.

Out of thin air, pieces start materializing. Large metallic plates. Pistons. Gatling guns. Then pieces that appear organic. Leathery lizard skin. Claws. Teeth.

Within seconds it's over and The Controller's creation is assembled, with him in the center of it, encased in steel. It stands over a hundred feet tall and is a monstrosity. Like Frankenstein's monster mixed with a tank. It stands upright on two robotic legs. One arm is a cannon, while the other is a claw with metal razor-sharp fingernails. Its head, if you could even call it that, is the worst part of it all. It's covered in skin that looks like it came from an alligator. Where its mouth should be there is a beak instead. From the eyes to the top of it's head, is all metal. Its pupil-less eyes glow a bright, vivid red.

After all the parts are in place, it releases a blood-curdling scream. Half beast, half machine, it towers over me. The Gatling gun, that is its left arm, begins to whir and I realize that I'm standing on the wrong side of it. The bullets miss me by inches as I run down the street, trying to put some distance between me and it, but I can hear it lumbering after me, shaking the entire city with each step.

Rounding the corner, I hover into the air and wait for it.

I've never had to fight anything this enormous, but I can't keep running.

As it rounds the corner, but before it's turned to face me, I take off heading straight for its head as fast as I can fly. It turns just in time to see me smash into it right between the eyes. This knocks the creature back, and it stumbles to regain its balance. That was close, but I need to hit it harder.

I turn in the air and head back towards it, this time from behind. I strain as I push myself to fly faster and faster. This time, I need to knock it over.

I can see its claw heading towards me in slow motion but even then, it's moving too quickly for me to react. It has me in its grip and begins digging its fingernails into my abdomen. Once again, I concentrate on cold and the claw begins freezing. It releases me before the claw fully turns to ice. He's learning. I fly straight up into the air to give myself space for another attack.

I hear the click of an engine behind me, followed by the sound of flames. It sounds like a space shuttle taking off, and it turns out that that's not to far from the truth as the beast begins its ascent towards me. Even the sky isn't safe from this thing, which I should have known. The Controller's creations are limited only by his own imagination, and the idea that this thing can fly isn't all that imaginative.

The Gatling gun whirs into action again and soon, I'm doing the best evasive maneuvers I can think of to avoid being caught by one of the projectiles. My maneuvers aren't evasive enough though. One of the bullets hits me. It must be the size of a fist. A very large man's fist. It hasn't pieced my skin, but it has knocked the wind out of my lungs.

I'm falling fast.

Hitting the ground hurts almost as much as the bullet. What's happening? I look at the metaband on my right arm and bring up the battery indicator. It's low. Very low. The lowest I've ever seen it.

Down the block, The Controller and his massive armor

descend.

"Come on!" The Controller's amplified voice beckons through the mechanized suit. "If you're supposed to be the most powerful of the new wave of metas, this is going to get very boring for me, very quickly."

I can't fight something this big. My training didn't prepare me for anything other than punching and kicking thugs. Not taking down monsters the size of skyscrapers. Even if my bands weren't almost completely depleted, I don't even know how to approach this thing.

Whatever my plan is going to be, I need to come up with it quickly. These metabands are critically low, and I don't know what happens when the battery gets down to zero.

I'm reminded of the battle between The Governor and Jones. The last large scale battle the world saw between two metas, before today. The day the entire world watched two metas die. One good, and one evil. They also saw something a meta had never done before: release pure energy from its metabands. It was the most extreme display of unadulterated power ever demonstrated by a meta. Jones used it to literally slice buildings in half, including the one my parents were in.

It's a long shot, but it's the only shot I have right now. The beast, that The Controller is inside, once again begins lumbering towards me. I think back to how I froze the snake, using an ability I didn't know I had before. If I truly am one of the most powerful metas, then maybe there are other abilities I haven't tapped yet, and maybe the ability to focus energy out of these bands like Jones could is one of them. Maybe it's not, but it's worth a try. I'm dead either way, if I don't.

The Controller is laughing. A loud, boisterous laughter through whatever machination inside that *thing* is amplifying his voice. He's marching this thing towards me. To finish me off.

I think back to the footage of Jones blasting through those buildings, his power seeming limitless. I close my eyes and focus on this image. With my eyes closed, I can hear a quiet, faint hum. I open my eyes and see that my metabands are glowing, ever so slightly. I concentrate harder and the glow intensifies. It's a yellowish glow, the color of the sun itself. The Controller's beast hesitates with its next step. Surely, he's seen the same footage I have a million times. He is obsessed with metas. He knows what this glowing leads to. It's flight or fight for him right now. Either turn and run to maybe face me another day, or come at me with everything he's got and hope to finish the job before I can fully unleash this new ability.

He chooses the latter.

This makes me very happy.

The beast begins to break into a runner's stride. Its gun whirring into action again. Its red, dead eyes locked onto me. It's close now, but I wait. I wait until it's almost on top of me, then I point both fists at it and think "release".

The blast is unlike anything I've ever seen in real life before. It bores a hole clean through the beast. Even though its face doesn't have the ability to convey emotion, it still seems surprised. You'd be surprised too, if something a hundredth your size just put a hole through your chest.

Inside the hole, I can see The Controller. He survived the blast, but is badly injured. With my last ounce of strength, I leap into the air, aiming for the crater I created inside the beast's chest. I aim perfectly, tackling The Controller as we both fall through the back of the creature and onto the pavement below.

Behind me, I can hear the beast fall forward onto the city street. Dead. Or whatever the equivalent is for these creations. Within a few seconds, it's completely disappeared, leaving behind a large impact crater where it landed face first into the ground.

There's debris and smoke in the air all around me, and I've lost sight of The Controller. I begin to get back on my feet, when I feel a searing pain in my right side. Looking down at it, I see a huge gash through my uniform, and more crucially, skin. There's a good deal of blood, but I'll live. I must have caught it on the edge of the hole I burned through the metallic beast. Normally this wouldn't have even happened in the first place, or would have at least healed by now, but a glance at my metaband shows that my battery charge is completely gone. The bands are essentially in standby mode. Enough power to keep the uniform intact thankfully, but little else.

The pain in my side is quickly replaced by a new pain emanating from the back of my skull as I fall to my knees. The Controller stands over me with a pipe. Part of the wreckage we've both created, I'm sure. He raises it again to bash me. Right before it reaches my face, I catch it with my right hand and pull it away. Turns out there was more power left in these things than I gave them credit for. The Controller backs away, frightened, no doubt, that I'm not nearly as dead as he'd hoped. He paws at his own metaband. I can see one small, red light. The same as mine.

"Well, it would appear neither of us are in any condition to finish this little skirmish today are we?" he says.

"That's not surprising to hear from someone so worthless," I say, still lying on the ground.

"Ohhh. So tough! You sound like one of them already. No, unfortunately I have no interest in engaging in a slap fight with you, while we wait for some opportunistic meta to come in here to steal either of our glories. Until next time," The Controller says as he begins to turn to walk away from me. He doesn't notice that I've stopped listening to him, and that I'm looking through him, down the street. He doesn't notice the look of terror on my face, that I'm not even thinking about trying to conceal.

He doesn't notice Jones walking towards us.

The Controller is startled at first, as anyone would be when they think they're in an empty city and someone's snuck up behind them. Even more so, when that person is the strongest meta the world's ever known. Especially when they're supposed to be dead.

"J...J...Jones?" The Controller barely stutters out.

"You!" I scream out. I try to make my way to my feet, but they cannot cooperate and betray me. I fall back to the ground.

The man who killed my parents continues his slow, confident walk towards the two of us. His face is emotionless. His eyes vacant. He's wearing a dark blue, three-piece business suit. Polished leather dress shoes. His angular face is clean-shaven and not a brunette hair on his head is out of place. He looks more like a fashion magazine model than a war criminal.

There's nothing left in my metabands. Nothing left when I need it the absolute most. When I can right the wrong that he did. Or at the very least, avenge it.

"Controller," Jones says in a slow, even tone.

"I can't believe it's you! Oh my God! This is incredible! Everyone thought you were..," The Controller says before Jones finishes his sentence.

"Dead?" he says. "No. Not dead. More alive than ever. Better than alive. And I've been watching you."

"You have?" The Controller no longer sounds like a villain as much as he does a fanboy.

"Yes, I have. I believe I can help you," Jones says, motioning towards The Controller's nearly depleted metabands. "You do want to finish this job, don't you?"

The Controller looks back at me.

"More than anything, sir," he says.

"Good. Deactivate your metabands, and I can recharge them for you, then you can finish this properly," Jones says.

"You can do that?" The Controller asks.

"There are many, many things I can do that you cannot even begin to fathom," Jones says.

"You don't want to kill him yourself, sir? I know that that was something you enjoyed too," The Controller says.

Jones stares through him. He is growing impatient.

"It's just that, if I deactivate the bands, he'll see me. The real me," The Controller says.

"And how will that matter once he's dead?" Jones asks.

"I guess so, it's just..," The Controller begins, but Jones interrupts him.

"It appears I've made a mistake," Jones says, as he turns and begins walking away.

"No! Wait! I'm sorry. You're right. I want this. I want to do this. I want to kill him, and I want you to help me. It would be such an honor for you to help me!" The Controller yells out after Jones.

Jones stops walking but does not turn around. He simply stands with his back to both of us and waits.

The Controller brings his fists up to his chest and clicks his metabands together. He brings his arms back down to his sides, and his suit retreats into the bands. Before me, no longer stands a tall, muscular male form. In its place is a short, squat, overweight, balding, man with an unkempt goatee. He looks like the stereotype of the person working behind the counter at a comic book store. I don't know what I expected from someone so depraved and obsessed with the darkest aspects of metahumans.

"Ha! This, this is the 'great and powerful' Controller?" I laugh at him. This enrages him, which is what I expect and what I want. He races towards me with the rage of someone who's been tormented in the past. I might not have much power left in these bands, but whatever is left is more than enough to at least break the arm of a non-metahuman. If all of this is going to be over for me in a few minutes, I at least want to leave him a token to remember me by.

"Stop," Jones says. The Controller freezes in his tracks. "That's what he wants you to do."

The Controller turns his back to me and walks back towards Jones.

"I'm sorry, sir. My anger got the best of me. There's so

much I can learn from you. You're right. I need my powers to finish him off correctly, even in his weakened state," The Controller says to Jones.

"Yes. You do. Now let me help you with that," Jones says.

"Of course. But how?" The Controller asks.

Jones places his hands on The Controller's metabands and stares him deep in the eyes.

"By letting go. Release these bands from your control, and I can transfer a fraction of the limitless power I contain in mine into yours," Jones says.

The Controller seems unsure, but in the end he relents to Jones. To his hero.

"Okay," The Controller says. He closes his eyes and Jones slowly, steadily slips the metabands off of The Controller's wrists. Once they are completely off, Jones disappears right before both of our eyes.

The Controller is confused, but tries not to show it. You can tell from his nervousness, that he's not quite sure what has just happened. He admires Jones. More than admires. Worships. But anyone who knows Jones, knows that he is nothing if not deceitful. There isn't much Jones can do with someone else's metabands though. They're still unbreakably tied to The Controller's DNA. They cannot be used by anyone else, under any other circumstances. But then again, I wasn't aware that one could transfer energy from their own bands into those of another and from the looks of it, The Controller didn't know this either.

Suddenly, Jones appears before both of us again. He's grinning. The first real show of emotion he's exhibited. The Controller smiles with him. There's a look of relief on his face.

"Ha, for a second there I thought you'd run away with my metabands!" The Controller jokes awkwardly.

Jones expression remains unchanged. A huge, grinning smile.

"Soooo, what now?" The Controller asks after an

uncomfortably long silence.

"Now? Nothing," Jones says, still grinning ear to ear.

"Wh... what do you mean nothing?" The Controller stutters out. "Where are my metabands?"

"Where are your metabands? Somewhere where you will never, ever see them again," Jones says.

"What?" The Controller says, his voice cracking. He is on the verge of tears. "What have you done with them?"

"I've just told you. I've put them somewhere where you will never find them. You're done, Controller," Jones says.

"You can't do that! You can't!" The Controller screams. "Those are mine! Those are my metabands! You can't just take them from me! Why would you do something like that, I thought we were friends!"

"We are anything but friends, you human garbage," Jones says.

The Controller is in a state of shock. He's been betrayed by his hero and lost his metabands all at the same time. He is practically in hysterics.

"I'll find them! I'll do whatever it takes, and I'll find them. Mark my words. I don't care if I have to scour the entire Earth, I *will* find my metabands again, and then you'll be sorry!" The Controller screams, his anger blinding him to the fact that Jones could snap his neck like a twig right now if he wanted to.

"Scouring the Earth to find your metabands isn't going to do you much good," Jones says. There's something happening. His facial features are changing. His clothes moving on their own.

Jones is no longer standing before either of us.

Iris is.

"Because your metabands aren't on Earth. They're on Mars," Iris says.

"What?" The Controller stammers out in confusion. For once, we're both in the same boat of not knowing what the hell is going on.

"Mars. That's where I put them. To be honest, they're not buried very deep, I never was that good at holding my breath but nevertheless, I still think you'll have a pretty hard time finding them," Iris says.

Iris was holding out on me. She never told me she could shapeshift. Seems she has a legitimate gripe for me getting credit for being the meta with the most varied abilities after all.

"You can't do this to me! You can't! I'll find a way! I promise you, I will find a way and you will be sorry! You think Silver Island can hold me? I'm The Controller! I will have my revenge, I swear to you!" he screams.

"Silver Island? That's for metahumans. You're going to state lock-up like the rest of the regular scum," a voice from behind me says.

It's Midnight. He's alive.

"Midnight!" I can't help myself from yelling out. "I thought you were..."

"You don't give me enough credit," he says.

The Controller sees what he thinks is an opportunity in our little family reunion and tries to make a run for it. Iris rolls her eyes. He's not very fast. Midnight lets him get about halfway down the block before he throws a bolo in his direction. The bolo whips down the street a foot above the ground and catches The Controller's legs, wrapping them up instantly. He falls to the ground hard enough to knock himself unconscious.

"That'll hold him until the police get here," Midnight says.

"But, how did you..," I begin to say.

"I'll explain everything, but first we need to get out of here or else, me and you are going to be joining him in a holding cell. Iris, do you have enough juice left to get us out here?" Midnight asks.

"Aww, for you guys? Of course," Iris says as she grabs both of us by the wrist and teleports us out of there.

THIRTY-SEVEN

I came to find out after the fact that Midnight and Iris' plan was set from the start. I didn't even know that they knew each other, but of course I didn't. Midnight isn't exactly forthcoming about his friends and aside from the whole crime-fighting thing, I didn't think he got out all that much.

Midnight had surveilled the apartment where The Controller was supposedly hiding in advance, that much I'd already known. What I hadn't known was that when Midnight first entered the apartment days ago, he found a crudely built pipe bomb already in place, rigged to explode whenever the door was opened for the next and last time. You had to give The Controller credit: he was actually one step ahead of Midnight. The only problem is; that Midnight is usually three or four steps ahead of even himself, so it doesn't do you much good.

He'd already had a deep psychological analysis of The Controller done when the attacks had first started. It was easy, considering there were years of blog posts, forums rants, etc. all under The Controller's online alias. Ultimately though, it didn't take a PhD in psychology to figure out what, or rather who, could get The Controller to lay down his arms: Jones.

Of course, procuring a dead man is difficult, even for Midnight. It's also inadvisable if said dead man is also responsible for war crimes that bordered on genocide. Which is why I was kept out of the plan. Midnight wasn't sure if I would be on board with the idea of resurrecting the image of the man who murdered half my family just to catch The Controller. He was sure that I would insist there was another way, or if push came to shove, simply refuse to be a part of it at all. He wasn't wrong. Seeing Jones, even if it wasn't actually *him,* brought about emotions that I hadn't felt in a long time. Emotions that I thought my metabands could protect me from ever feeling again.

Iris was the only meta that Midnight knew who could shapeshift, an ability I didn't even know she possessed, but this wasn't the first time I'd be surprised that Midnight knew something I didn't. He sought her out and talked her into going along with his crazy plan, making her promise not to say a word of it to me.

Neither understood or knew how powerful I was or could be. Their plan was risky, which was why it was a plan B all along. Plan A was for me to simply beat The Controller. It was something that Midnight thought I might have been ready to do on my own. I couldn't. It's made me doubt just how unique my abilities truly were, if at the end of the day, I still couldn't even defeat the thirty-seven year-old loner who lived in his mom's basement and subsisted on a diet of pizza and cola.

But Midnight insists that he still believes in me. He's also lied to me in the past.

I still don't know what to make of Iris. That night she teleported us back to the city and in another instant, she was gone again. Even Midnight seemed confused by that. I haven't seen her since.

It's quiet now. And that's good. When I was a kid, I dreamed of being a meta just like every other kid before The Battle. Possessing that kind of power and being able to do almost anything. In reality, the responsibility is terrifying, and inescapable. These metabands are bonded to me, and only me, until the day I die or they turn off, whichever comes first. And as long as I have them, I'll never know which of those days is coming for me first.

"Hey. Space cadet. I don't want to tell you how to do your job or anything, but I'm pretty sure you're supposed to tie up those garbage bags once you pull them out of the can, not just stare inside them for five minutes," Sarah says behind me.

I'm at the lake, at work, but obviously my mind is

anywhere but.

"There's a method to all of this. You wouldn't know the first thing about it, to be honest," I say to her, kidding.

"Sorry. I forgot you're a waste *engineer*. I'm just a lowly life*guard*," she says.

"Exactly! I'm so glad you see it the same way I do! All I'm saying is don't forget your place. Engineers always trump lowly *guards*," I say as I tie up the garbage bag which I now realize is unbelievably disgusting smelling, even for garbage.

"I'm so sorry, *sir,*" Sarah says with a smile.

"It's alright. I'll let it slide. This time. But I've got my eye on you."

"Actually, I think I noticed that."

Oh no. Am I flirting? Was my being a smartass, actually unintentional flirting? Is that all flirting is? Why didn't anyone tell me this sooner! I could have been doing stuff like this all along, barring the whole 'being scared to death of talking to girls thing' I guess.

Wait. More importantly, much more importantly: is she flirting back? I'm taking too much time to think about this, and now she thinks I'm being weird. Say something. Anything.

"Yeah?" I say.

Great job, idiot.

Sarah laughs. It actually almost sounds like a nervous laugh. That can't be though, right? She's gorgeous, smart, funny and all around amazing. Girls like that don't get nervous. Right?

"Sorry, that was stupid. I tend to stick my foot in my mouth sometimes," she says.

"What? No. Of course that's not stupid. Of course I've got my eye on you. I'd be crazy not too. Annnnd now, I'm the one who stuck his foot in his mouth," I say.

Sarah laughs. There's still a slight nervousness behind it, but it seems like at least a little bit a laugh of relief too.

"All right, look, I'm just going to ask before this gets

anymore unnecessarily awkward for either of us. Would you... and you can totally say no, seriously, it's not big deal, but would you possibly ever be interested in maybe seeing a movie together sometime?" she asks me.

"Seriously?" I ask back.

"Sorry, like I said you can totally say no, I probably..."

"I'd love to."

"Really?"

"Of course."

"Great! I mean, cool," she says, trying to hide what I think is actual excitement. "Are you doing anything tonight?"

"No, not at all."

"Perfect. What about that new movie 'Horses on a Plane'? I know it sounds stupid but..."

"Stupid? That sounds absolutely horrifying! What if one of them got spooked and decided to kick out one of the windows?" I say.

"Exactly! That totally happens in the trailer! The movie trailer that is, not the horse trailer. I think they're actually pretty calm whenever they're in the horse trailer, but I don't know about these horses. They've been infected with some type of zombie disease as they're being flown on a commercial flight to the big horse race down in Kentucky...," she says.

I've stopped listening. The girl, who I think is the most amazing girl I've ever met, is geeking out over a horror movie to me, a horror movie that we're actually going to see together, as in a date, and I'm not listening. It's not because I'm rude. It's because something else has grabbed my attention.

It's the sky. It's lit up. Dozens of lights, all streaking down from the sky. Maybe hundreds. Like comets entering the Earth's atmosphere. Sarah slowly realizes that I'm not listening to her anymore and turns to look at what has grabbed my attention.

"Whoa. What is that?" she asks.

"I don't know,"

Now the majority of the lake goers are staring into the sky as well, asking the same question, when someone comes running up to the beach and pulls an earbud out from their ear.

"They're metabands! The news is saying there are reports coming in from all over the world! Hundreds of metabands are falling from the sky!"

Before my brain has time to even process the words coming from this man's mouth, I can feel my phone buzzing in the pocket of my shorts. I pull it out, but it takes a moment before I can pull my eyes away from the sky to read the message.

"HQ. NOW! - M." It reads.

"Sarah," I say.

"Uh huh," she replies, unable to unfix her gaze from the sky either.

"I might have to take a rain check on tonight..."

Social Media and Internet Things

Thank you so much for taking the time read my book. If you enjoyed it and would like to leave a review about it on whatever Internet website you bought it from it would mean the absolute world to me and make sure that there's more. If you bought the book at an actual store, wow. I guess you can go to the store and tell the nice man or woman that sold it to you how much you enjoyed it.

Book 2 is coming Summer 2014. For more information please visit http://tomreynolds.com/book2

To stay in the loop on all things 'Meta' and otherwise with me, please sign up for my mailing list at http://tomreynolds.com/list. No spam, I promise.

You can find my online elsewhere at the following, or you can email me at tom@tomreynolds.com. Don't be a stranger!

Internet: http://tomreynolds.com
Twitter: http://twitter.com/tomreynolds
Instagram: http://twitter.com/tomreynolds
Facebook: https://www.facebook.com/sometomreynolds
Podcast: http://tcgte.com

Acknowledgements

First and foremost, thank you to my Mom, Dad and brother Ryan. They've been my sounding board my entire life and have always been more sure of myself than I ever have. This book would have never been finished without their encouragement.

Thanks to Tim Daniels for pushing me creatively, every week, for four years now on The Complete Guide to Everything. I've always found that the hardest part of doing anything creative is actually *doing* it, but having Tim push me for so long again made it possible for this book to be written.

Thank you to my editor Laura Kingsley who did a great job deciphering the mess of the first drafts I gave her to get them to the point where you're here and have presumably finished the book.

Extra special thanks to cover artist Damon Za whose amazing work was the final, extra hard kick in the ass I needed to get this out of me. He's been extremely generous with his time and talent and helped inspire me to make this book as good as I possibly could.

Finally thank you to everyone who bought this because you know me from The Complete Guide to Everything. All hyperbole aside, I really think we have the best, most supportive listeners a podcast could ever ask for. Knowing that there would at least be someone besides my friends and family to show this to when I was done was the best motivation I could ever have, and that would have never been the case without you guys, so thanks.

About the Author

Tom Reynolds graduated from The University of Maryland - College Park with a Bachelor of Arts in American Studies, where he also accidentally minored in English. He lives in Brooklyn, NY with a dog named Ginger who despite being illiterate proved to be a really great late night writing partner.